The Demon
in the
Embers

Julia Edwards was born in 1977. She lives in Salisbury with her husband and three sons, and sometimes feels outnumbered.

The Demon in the Embers is the fourth book in *The Scar Gatherer* series, seven adventure novels about time-travel. To find out more, please visit: *www.scargatherer.co.uk*.

Also by Julia Edwards

The Leopard in the Golden Cage
Saving the Unicorn's Horn
The Falconer's Quarry

For adults

Time was Away

THE FOURTH BOOK IN The Scar Gatherer SERIES

The Demon in the Embers

Julia Edwards

For Freddie,
Best wishes,
Julia Edwards

Published in the United Kingdom by:

Laverstock Publishing
129 Church Road, Laverstock, Salisbury,
Wiltshire, SP1 1RB, UK

First printed September 2016

Cover design by Peter O'Connor
www.bespokebookcovers.com

ISBN: 978-0-9928443-6-3

For more information about the series, please visit
www.scargatherer.co.uk

For Christopher,
my own little firebird

ACKNOWLEDGEMENTS

I am still deeply grateful to my husband and my parents for their support and belief in *The Scar Gatherer*. My map of Lucy's London owes a great deal to several wonderful maps by the late Reginald Piggott, and I was delighted to discover Liza Picard's incredible collection of facts about Restoration London, including the turkeys and the hair remover. My greatest thanks, however, go to Tamsin Lewis, who, having checked the manuscript of the previous book in the series, boldly offered to check this one as well. Her input has once again been invaluable. Thanks also go to the children and staff of Winterbourne Earls Primary School who cheered me on through the writing of this book, and spotted quite a few errors in the draft version. As ever, any mistakes that remain are my own.

LUCY'S

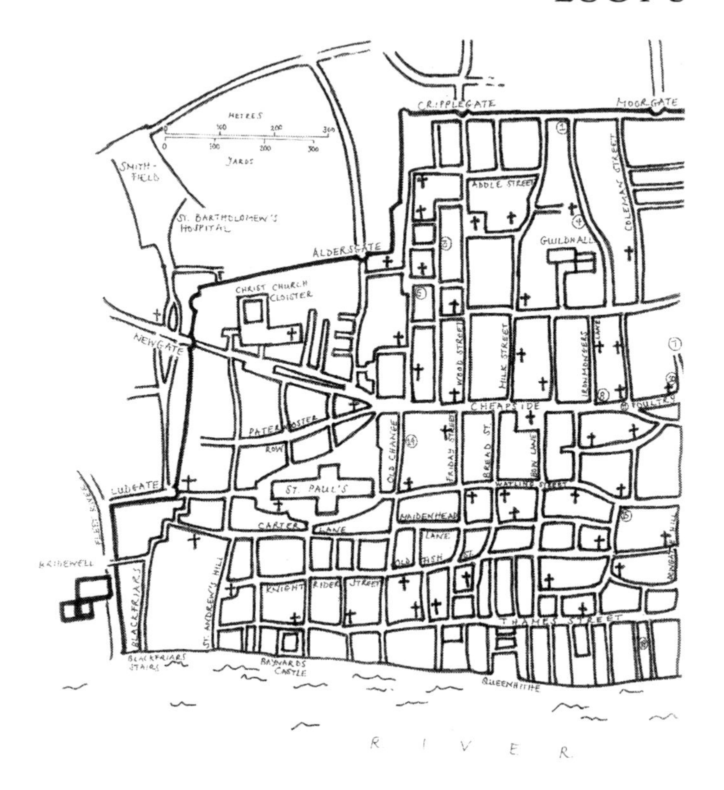

1 Masons' Hall
2 Carpenters' Hall
3 Haberdashers' Hall
4 Coopers' Hall
5 Goldsmiths' Hall
6 Lucy's house
7 Grocers' Hall
8 Mercers' Hall
9 Royal Exchange
10 General Letter Office

LONDON

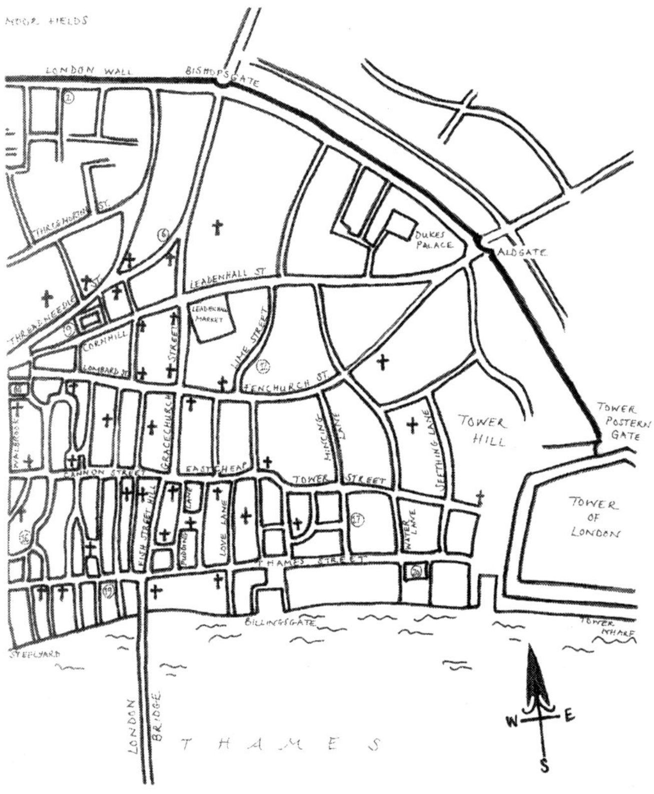

11 Great Conduit
12 Pewterers' Hall
13 Stocks Market
14 St. Paul's School
15 Cutlers' Hall
16 Plumbers' Hall
17 Bakers' Hall
18 Whittington's Longhouse
19 Fishmongers' Hall
20 Customs House

1

Joe followed the tour party across the gravel. Ahead of them, the guide stopped.

"When people think of the Tower of London," the guide said, "they think of torture and execution. But in fact, it was a palace and a fortress."

Quietly, Joe unzipped the pocket of his shorts and slipped his hand in. He felt a flutter of panic. What if his St. Christopher had fallen out? It was risky, bringing it to London. But if he wanted to slip through time, he had to have it with him. And he couldn't wear it around his neck, because then he couldn't drop it.

But it was still there, safely in his pocket. Joe's pulse settled. He wound his fingers through the chain. In fact, the Tower wasn't going to be a good place to drop it, he'd realised, after he and Mum had bought their tickets and come in. If he did manage to slip through time here, he'd have terrible trouble getting out.

"Very few people were actually executed at the

Tower," the guide was saying. "The most famous is probably Anne Boleyn, the second wife of Henry the Eighth, who was beheaded on the spot where we're now standing. Wife number five, Catherine Howard, was also executed here, and so was another queen a few years later, Lady Jane Grey. She was only sixteen."

"This is a jolly day out!" Mum murmured in Joe's ear. He glanced round. She was smiling.

It *was* a jolly day out, just the two of them, doing something together other than being shuffled around hospital departments, while the doctors failed to find anything wrong with Joe.

There wasn't anything wrong, of course. It was just that his body was struggling more and more to adjust each time he slipped in and out of Lucy's worlds. It had been a couple of months now since he last saw Lucy at Old Wardour Castle, so naturally he hadn't had any more episodes. But it would happen again, he was certain.

He knew it would make his life easier if there was nobody there to watch. But to get into Lucy's next world, he had to be in the right place in his own one. So far, that had always meant being where other people were. Even so, this really was the wrong place.

"The other famous executions took place on Tower Hill," the guide went on. "Thomas More, Thomas Cromwell, and so on. Of course, it was big business in its day, executing people. Huge crowds came to watch, not unlike Wimbledon maybe – although Andy Murray should still have his head on his shoulders when he comes off court this afternoon, even if he loses the match!"

Around Joe, some of the other tourists in the group chuckled. Joe bit his lip. He'd always watched the tennis with Dad. But last summer, Wimbledon had been on in the background while Dad packed his things and moved out. Joe hadn't watched any of it this year.

He felt Mum squeeze his shoulder, as though she knew what he was thinking. It had been her suggestion that they come up to London and do some sightseeing, to make the most of Joe's brother, Sam, being away at scout camp.

"The Tower was also home to the Royal Menagerie for over six hundred years," the guide continued. "It started with King John who kept lions and bears here. His son, Henry the Third, was given a wedding gift of three lions or three leopards, we're not sure which. And later on, James the First had a platform built so that he could watch his lions fighting the other animals."

"Horrible man!" Mum whispered. "It would have served him right if Guy Fawkes *had* blown him up!"

But Joe wasn't really listening. He was thinking about the leopard which had been given to Lucy's family when he'd met her at Fishbourne Roman

Palace. After what had happened there, he could see how keeping such dangerous animals might cause problems.

"What happened to the Royal Menagerie?" someone asked. "Why isn't it still here?"

The guide raised an eyebrow. "Space," he said. "The animals apparently found it cramped – there were quite a few escapes and several attacks. In the 1830s, they were moved to Regent's Park, to what's now London Zoo."

"Would you like to go to the zoo this afternoon?" Mum asked Joe, when they were standing outside the Tower a while later.

Joe thought about it. It seemed a bit of a wasted opportunity when they could equally well go to Marwell or Bristol.

What he really wanted was to find the right place to drop his St. Christopher, to try and see Lucy again. Almost anywhere around London might work, as long as his feet were touching the ground. It had worked like that in York after all. Of course, he had no idea whether Lucy had actually lived in London at any time, but there was only one way to find out.

"Let's have lunch first and decide after that," he said. "We could go to one of those cafés over there."

As they walked along the road towards them, he unzipped his pocket again and held the St. Christopher in his hand. He wondered if he could drop it without Mum noticing. It wouldn't be easy. The pavement wasn't that crowded, and the traffic was streaming past. If the St. Christopher rolled into the road, he might never get it back.

Then he had an idea. If he pretended to retie his shoelace, he could press the St. Christopher to the ground without letting go of it. He wouldn't be able to do that more than twice without Mum getting suspicious. But it was better than nothing.

Before she could turn around, he stooped down and let the pendant of the St. Christopher touch the pavement.

A taxi whizzed past. But the hissing in Joe's ears grew louder as the taxi got further away. He held his breath.

The hissing grew and grew. His heart began to pound. He'd done it! It had worked! His skin tingled with excitement and alarm. There was no going back now!

The world swung round. His fingers were still moving, pretending to fiddle with his laces. But his trainers were gone.

He blinked and waited for the dizziness to pass. Thank goodness it wasn't so bad going this way, from his world into Lucy's.

As the spinning stopped, the shoes he was now wearing came into focus. They were made of dull, black leather, clumsily cut, and they came to square points at the front. Woollen stockings stretched up to his knees, and above them was something like a pair of baggy shorts. They were brownish green and made of thick, scratchy material, not at all like the shorts he'd been wearing in his own world. These might be breeches, he thought. He'd have to find out later.

When he was sure he wasn't dizzy any more, he straightened up. He steadied himself against the building next to him, keeping his hand tightly closed around his St. Christopher.

The street was cobbled, though dirt filled most of the gaps around the stones. It was very narrow, only just wide enough for two carts to pass each other, and there were no pavements. The buildings jutted out overhead from both sides, and in some places, the upper storeys almost touched in the middle, blocking out all but a strip of smoky blue sky.

A shout right in front of Joe made him jump. It was a man pushing a barrow with what looked like sacks of coal. He didn't seem to be shouting at anyone in particular. People pushed past in both directions: children carrying packages, two gentlemen on horseback, a woman leading a donkey, knocking on doors. At one house, she stopped to milk the animal. Joe stared. He'd never seen a donkey being milked!

A horse and carriage plodded by, unable to go any faster than the people on foot, and women with trays of strawberries and raspberries wove in and out. A pair of ragged boys dawdled past, kicking a stone from one to the other, and a man rolled a barrel along, calling out something that sounded like sand. Was that what the shouting meant, Joe wondered, traders advertising their wares? But then, what about the old man who didn't seem to be carrying anything? He was calling out something that almost had a tune. Joe watched, baffled. Then the door of a house opened and a woman came out with a bundle of knives. The man took a whetstone from his pocket and began to sharpen them.

Joe couldn't decide whether it was the people or the noise that was most bewildering. Besides the shouting of the streetsellers, there was the clatter of hooves and the grinding of wheels as a horse and cart rumbled over the cobbles. Bells were ringing, the signs hanging from the buildings squeaked in the breeze, and there was the piercing, clacking noise of something like a football rattle. Small children wailed and dogs darted in and out, barking or yelping when they got kicked. From the house behind Joe came the trill of a bird, and the sound of a violin drifted out of another window.

He jumped a second time as the clash of a hammer on an anvil started up very nearby. He turned around, but couldn't see a blacksmith anywhere. It must be in the yard next to one of these buildings. Workshops, shops and houses seemed to be all mixed up together.

There was a terrible stink of smoke, rubbish, rotting meat and sewage, not unlike how it had been in

Jorvik. But there was also a bitter, metallic smell, and something acrid burning. Joe tried to remember whether he'd ever got used to the smells in Jorvik. He didn't think so.

He was uncomfortably hot, he realised. The air here was much warmer than it had been at home. He put his hand to his collar to loosen it.

But where he'd been wearing a T-shirt before, he now had a jacket made of the same thick material as the shorts, buttoned all the way up to his chin. No wonder he was stifling! The sleeves stopped just below his elbows, and a shirt stuck out over his forearms, finishing in long, grubby frills at his wrists. The same shirt was also billowing out around his waist, between the jacket and shorts. Joe thought of Mum's daily reminders to tuck himself in before he went to school. She would have a fit at this!

At the collar of the jacket hung two white strips of material. He squinted down at them. These, too, were slightly dirty looking. He fastened his St. Christopher around his neck and tucked it down inside his shirt. It would have to stay there until he could give it to Lucy, assuming he found her!

On his head was a dark, wide-brimmed hat which seemed to be curled up slightly on one side. That would be good for keeping the sun off, he supposed, since there wouldn't be any sunglasses here! He chortled inwardly at the idea. But of course, if the streets were all as narrow and overhung as this one, he wouldn't ever see the sun anyway.

There was another yell, this time from a carter cracking his whip to drive his horse through the crowds. Joe shrank back. The metal rims of the wheels grated past, just centimetres from his toes. The driver carried on bawling abuse at the people ahead of him. A woman with a basket of fish on her head screeched back, and a man on horseback shouted and waved his fist. But the carter just cracked his whip again and drove on. By the time the cart was gone, flies already covered the steaming heap of dung the horse had left behind.

Joe set off up the street, looking at the houses as he went. The walls were mostly made with wooden beams filled in with white or mustard-coloured plaster. Dad had told Joe once that this style was built by the Tudors. So perhaps he was in Tudor times again, he thought hopefully. If Lucy's family had moved from Old Wardour to London, he might be in the same world as last time, just a few months later. The clothes were different, it was true, but that might just be London fashions.

On the other hand, it could be another era altogether. After all, these buildings hadn't just been put up. They could have been here a hundred years or more. In fact, some of them looked a bit like they'd grown here, popping up in the tiniest gaps.

A lot of houses were three or even four storeys high, each level piled higgledy piggledy on top of the last, so that they looked as though they might fall over at any moment. And they were all wood and plaster. He couldn't see a single one made of brick or stone.

Suddenly, he was grabbed from behind.

"Got one!" yelled a man's voice just above Joe's ear. Joe's head jangled. The man shifted his grip, pinning Joe's arms to his sides.

Joe looked over his shoulder. A second man had emerged from the crowd. He was unshaven and heavy. "Too small!" he declared. "And too young, I reckon!"

The first man spun Joe round, making sure he didn't let go. He looked Joe up and down. "Healthy, though. I say we take him for the quota. If we get our twenty, he can be a bonus extra. And if we don't, at least we can count him in. I mean, we haven't exactly had much luck this morning, have we?"

Joe squirmed between the man's hands. They were rough, with dirt ingrained in the skin. The man tightened his hold. People were still going past, but nobody paid the slightest attention.

"What'll we do with him?" asked the second man, still dubious. "Take him down to Bridewell to be locked up with the rest?"

"Quicker to take him straight to the ship," said the first, jerking his head towards a side street. "It's only a stone's throw. They can set him to work right away."

"Then he won't count as one of ours," objected the second man.

"Don't worry about that. I'll make sure he does!"

The first man swung Joe round to face away from him again and gave him a shove. Joe stumbled forward down the side street, trying frantically to think what to do. He hadn't yet got his bearings in this new world. But if he didn't try and escape from these men right now, he'd soon be doing something he'd much rather not.

He sank his teeth into the hand of the man holding him. The man yelled and loosened his grip. Taking his chance, Joe wrenched one arm free, twisted round and punched the man in the groin. The man roared.

But as Joe scrambled away from him, he slipped on the cobbles. At once, the second man leapt on him. An enormous fist hovered above Joe's face. Joe winced. He'd only just got here! He couldn't be pulled back into his own time yet. But if he wasn't, he'd be beaten to a pulp!

"Stop!" shouted another voice. "What on earth do you think you're doing?"

The man astride Joe paused. "What's it to you if I beat my own errand boy?" He glowered.

The man who had shouted strode towards them. His jacket flapped at his thighs, and ringlets of long, black hair bounced on his shoulders beneath an extravagant hat. "He's not your errand boy though, is he?" he snapped. "I recognise you and your friend. I've seen you a few times in the last week, pressing men for the ships. If our hopes of victory rest on boys as young as this one, the Dutch will have an easy time of it!"

Joe turned his head. The man who'd grabbed him was backing away.

"Let him go!" commanded the man with the ringlets. "Go and find someone who's at least big enough to put up a fight!"

Resentfully, the second man lumbered to his feet and stomped off. Joe let out a gasp.

His rescuer bent down and offered his hand. "Bad luck, young fellow!" he said. "They must be getting desperate if they'll take a boy like you."

"What for?" Joe panted. "What were they going to do with me?"

"They're seizing men to press."

Joe dusted himself down, wondering what on earth this meant.

The man must have realised he didn't understand, because he explained, "They'd have dragged you off to the quay and put you on a ship to go to war."

"War!" Joe's eyes widened. He didn't dare ask which war.

"Allow me to escort you home," the man said. "I don't want you to come to any more harm."

Joe pulled his hat straight. "I'm afraid I don't live here, sir," he said reluctantly. There were going to be enough lies he would have to tell, without adding unnecessary ones. "In fact, I've only just arrived."

"Come to London to seek your fortune, like my fellow mercer, Whittington?" the man asked wryly.

"Whittington?" Joe repeated.

"You must know the ballad."

Joe hesitated. Was he talking about Dick Whittington? Had Dick Whittington been real, then? And in that case, what was a mercer? In the fairy tale, he'd been Lord Mayor, hadn't he? But that wasn't the same thing, Joe was sure.

Or had he blundered into some kind of fairy-tale world? It certainly didn't feel like it.

"Or are you escaping something?" the man asked. "You're alone, I presume."

Joe nodded.

"No parents?"

"No."

"What is it then, boy? We hear the plague still rages in the east of the country. Is that it? Have you fled the contagion and didn't want to say, in case I send you packing?"

Joe paused for a moment, then nodded again. If he was going to be given an explanation for why he was here, it would be foolish not to take it, even if he didn't quite understand.

"Your parents are dead? Poor boy!" the man said, taking Joe's reticence as agreement. "My wife and I lost four of our children last year, and a baby too, not a month old. It's brought misery beyond imagining."

Joe was silent. He didn't deserve this man's sympathy, but it was too late to tell him the truth now.

"Why don't you come home with me? I'm on my way back for dinner. You can eat with us and rest a while. You can stay a few days, if you wish. My wife and daughter will look after you. I have a son, too, not much older than you, I'd guess. How old are you?"

"Eleven, sir," Joe replied.

"Peter is thirteen. You might have things in common."

Joe looked up sharply. Peter had been the name of Lucy's brother. He should be thirteen now, or thereabouts.

Joe peered at the man's face beneath the curls and the plumed hat. Was this Lucy's father? He'd barely seen him at Old Wardour, and with the long, dark hair and these clothes, he looked completely different from how he'd looked in Jorvik.

"What's your name, boy?" the man asked.

"Joseph Hopkins, sir, though everyone calls me Joe."

"Very good, Joe." The man swept his hat from his head and bowed. "I'm glad to be of service. Now, come with me."

2

The man strode swiftly back up the street and turned left. He carried a walking cane, but it seemed to be for style, not support, even though his shoes had high heels, Joe noticed, which were surely difficult to walk on over the cobbles. Joe hurried along beside him, glad that his heels weren't high like that.

Although the man seemed kind, Joe felt anxious. Every other time he'd arrived in a new world, Lucy had been the first person he saw, or if not quite the first, still the first he'd spoken to. He hadn't realised how much he relied on meeting her straight away. But this time, he hadn't found her, and now he'd agreed to go with a stranger, somebody he hoped was her father, but who might very well not be. He thought how many times he'd been told not to talk to strangers, never to go with a stranger. His stomach knotted up. He'd gone against all the warnings!

Yet, what was the alternative? He couldn't very well just wander around in this foreign London, hoping to run into Lucy. It was clear that he didn't have a clue what dangers might lurk here, since he'd had to be rescued already. And it was foolish to hope that the one person he knew from the past would suddenly appear. There must be thousands of people living here, even tens or hundreds of thousands. He had no idea how big this city was. But he could see how unlikely it was that he would find Lucy even if she *was* here somewhere.

And what if she wasn't? It was a sudden and terrible thought. What if she didn't exist here at all? He'd taken it for granted that this was her latest world. But why shouldn't there be worlds in the past that didn't include her? Despite the heat, Joe shivered. All he could do was go with the man and hope for the best. It wasn't much of a plan, but he didn't have a better one.

As they walked, they kept to the side of the road as much as possible, beneath the overhanging buildings. There were empty baskets on the ground outside many of the houses, and more than once, Joe nearly tripped.

Most other people were trying to keep to the sides too, since the middle of the street was busy with horses, carriages, and carts that came dangerously close to colliding when they passed each other. Even when the road was clear, the centre of it was strewn with all kinds of rubbish, including bits of vegetables, sawdust, straw and ash, and of course, endless horse dung.

Here and there puddles of water trickled away through broken paving, or into a gully that ran down the middle of the road, though this was mostly blocked. Joe was just wondering where the water had come from, since it wasn't raining, when there was a shout from above. His companion stopped in his tracks. Joe stopped too.

From a window two storeys up, liquid sluiced down, splattering the middle of the street just ahead of them. Joe looked up in time to see a woman turning a large china potty the right way up. These puddles weren't water! They were wee! It was no wonder the place stank! Joe wondered whether they did this with poo as well. He hadn't noticed any, but decided to be more careful about where he put his feet.

Further along, the man turned right into a narrower street, and then at the end of this one, left again. Joe tried to keep track of the way they'd come, but he had no real sense of where they were, except that the Tower of London must be somewhere behind them, and the river too perhaps. He hoped it didn't matter. If this man *was* Lucy's father, in a short time, he would see Lucy again and be able to explore this new London with her. He knew from experience that the place would quickly start to feel more familiar with her at his side.

Then another terrible thought occurred to him. Even if this man *was* William Lucas, he'd said that four of his children had died of plague. What if Lucy had been one of them? He'd mentioned a daughter, but that could perfectly well be one of her sisters. There was no reason why Lucy should have survived rather than Anne or Cecily. Joe's stomach clenched even more tightly. He didn't want to be here without her!

Before he could think any further about it, however, he was distracted by a peculiar sound ahead. It wasn't quite like anything he'd heard before, even back at home, a sort of chuckling and whistling of many voices, gentle rather than shrill, but still loud in the narrow street. There was a strong smell, too, that reminded Joe of a farmyard.

"Oh dear," the man said, as they came to a halt behind a gathering crowd. "If he's hoping to get a good price for those, he's going to be disappointed."

Joe craned his neck to see what his companion was talking about. Beyond the people in front of them, the whole width of the street was filled by a soft blanket of greyish brown and black at about the height of Joe's thigh. It stretched right along the road as far as he could see, and was moving slowly forward, undulating as it went. It dawned on Joe that the forest of pink stalks sticking out of it were necks and heads. Even so, he still wasn't sure what he was looking at.

"Trade over at Newgate will have dropped off by now," the man said. "The white market does most of its business between five and about eight or nine. But it's nearly noon and he's got the whole city to get across. He'll be better off warehousing them till Saturday if he can, though he must have about a thousand birds there."

Joe was still puzzled.

"Unfortunately, they're not the most intelligent creatures, turkeys. If you try to hurry them, they get in a panic and it takes even longer."

Turkeys! Joe grinned. No wonder he hadn't recognised them! Who would expect to see a thousand turkeys on a London street?

"Where have they come from?" he asked, tentatively.

"Did you not see them on your way into London? They're usually driven in from Norfolk and Suffolk."

"By cart?" Joe asked.

The man burst out laughing. "No! On their own two feet, like they are now. Rearing turkeys doesn't make a man rich!"

Joe blushed.

"If the farmer's doing well, he might have shod them," the man added more gently. "They probably walk better in shoes."

"Shoes!" Joe echoed, before he could stop himself.

"Well, not quite shoes. That's geese. They have shoes to walk to market. The turkeys' feet are dipped in tar and sand, I think. Come on. It'll take us all day if we stay behind them. We'll turn back and go up Lime

Street."

Joe followed the man back through the big crowd that had now built up behind them. In a way, it was a bit like Jorvik on the day of the ship burial – another historic traffic jam! The place did remind him of Jorvik a little, especially the smell. But there was obviously much more wealth here. Almost all of the buildings they'd passed were a lot taller than any of the Jorvik houses had been, and there were diamond shaped panes of glass in most of the open windows. It was true, there were plenty of tumbledown houses that were scarcely better than hovels. But even they mostly had one upstairs floor, and between them were quite a few much grander dwellings, some of them with stained glass crests in their windows.

As they turned left onto another street, a beautiful carriage jolted past, drawn by horses with plumed head-dresses. The driver wore ornate livery, but no hat despite his head being bald. Joe wondered why. Everyone else he'd seen here, from the youngest to the oldest, was wearing some kind of hat or head covering, and most of the men had hair down to their shoulders, even if it wasn't as nicely curled as his companion's.

"Here we are!" the man said.

Joe looked up at the house they'd stopped at. Like so many others, it was built with black beams and white walls, sandwiched between its neighbours. The second and third storeys jutted out over the road. Part way up the wall of the second storey hung a sign, like the sign outside a pub. There were no words on it, no name, just a picture of some kind of exotic bird. Joe wondered what it meant. Perhaps the man kept a shop here. But Joe still couldn't guess from the sign what it might sell.

When they stepped inside, however, there was no shop or workshop, just a hallway. Before Joe's eyes could adjust to the gloom, a shape launched itself towards him from the top of a wall-hanging. He staggered backwards as it wrapped itself around his face, knocking his hat off. It was warm and furry. Joe grappled with it. A thin, hairy snake coiled around his neck. Panic mounted inside him. He couldn't loosen its grip! It was going to strangle him!

"Get off, Solomon!" barked the man. "Peter, would you come and get this animal please! It's too much for our visitors to be leapt on the moment they walk through the door!"

"He's upstairs," said a girl's voice. "Here, Solomon."

At once, the creature let go of Joe. He watched it spring onto the shoulder of the fair-haired girl who had come along the passage. It was a monkey, Joe saw, small and quite sweet when you weren't fighting it off.

The girl held something between thumb and finger, which the monkey was instantly intent on taking. Joe looked at the girl carefully, hoping to see some resemblance to Lucy. But there was none at all.

Dread grew inside him. Where Lucy was dark, this girl was blonde. Lucy had been about the same height as him, but this girl was shorter and plumper. Without doubt, this wasn't his friend. It wasn't even Cecily or Anne!

A woman appeared in the doorway behind the girl, carrying two dishes. Joe watched as she went past into the room on the left. Unlike the girl, she did look vaguely familiar, but she wasn't Lucy's mother.

"Solomon will do anything for a cherry," the girl said, smiling.

"Will he really?" The man's eyebrows went up. "How about sitting quietly on his stand for an hour without causing havoc?"

"But I only let him off the leash five minutes ago, when I came in," came a voice from above. "He can't stay tied up all day! He has to have some fun!" A fair-haired boy a bit older than Joe was coming down the stairs.

Joe looked up. Relief flooded his chest. This *was* Peter. His hair was longer than last time, and he'd grown taller, but Joe was certain it was him. He felt like hugging the other boy.

The girl let the monkey have the cherry. At once, it skipped onto Peter's shoulder where it sat, delicately nibbling the flesh of the fruit, stripping it from the stone. The girl turned and went back along the corridor to the room the woman had come from.

Joe's mind raced. What had happened to this

family? The man had said his son was called Peter. And this *was* the Peter Joe knew. So in that case, the man must be William Lucas after all. But if the girl was his daughter and the woman his wife … Had he remarried? He must have done. And that surely meant that Ellen was dead, and so too were Lucy, Cecily and Anne. Joe could hardly bear to think of it.

William Lucas picked up Joe's hat from the floor and put it with his own on a side table. Then, to Joe's astonishment, he lifted his hair off. It was a wig! Beneath it, his head was stubbly, as though his hair had been shaved off. He placed the wig on a stand, then took out an ornately embroidered skullcap from a drawer, and put it on.

"Alright," he said to his son. "Just make sure you clear up the poo this time. Don't disappear back to school pretending you've forgotten again!"

He turned to Joe. "Solomon is a macaque. I bought him from an Indian trader last time I was in Antwerp, to cheer us all up. But he's more trouble than he's worth! He's clearly very intelligent." At this, the monkey gave an ear-splitting shriek. "But he refuses to do his business in one place." William glared at the monkey. "Sometimes it smells almost as bad in here as it does out on the street! On balance, I think I preferred the sparrow Elizabeth tamed. It used to eat at the table with us, and it didn't make half as much mess."

Elizabeth. Joe's mouth formed the name soundlessly. That must be the girl. She must be

William Lucas' step-daughter. He swallowed.

William pushed open a door. Joe followed. The room they stepped into was only a little lighter than the hallway. It seemed to be a sort of sitting room, Joe thought, though it wasn't much like his own sitting room at home. There was a rug in the middle of polished floorboards, and a bench stood along one wall. To the side was a small table covered with a carpet, as the table at Old Wardour had been, and around it were three chairs with carved legs and tapestry cushions.

Facing the window, to catch what little light filtered in through the greyish panes, was an embroidery frame. A woman sat working at this. On the other side of the room from the door, a girl stood with her back to them in front of an elaborately painted rectangular box set on another table. She seemed to be playing it like a piano, because music tinkled from it.

Joe's pulse quickened again. *This* girl might be Lucy. She was the right height, and slender like his friend had been. But until he saw her face, he couldn't be sure.

"This is my wife and daughter," William said.

The woman and the girl both turned from what they were doing. Joe looked into familiar blue eyes. The tension that had been mounting inside him broke like a dam. He wanted to laugh. It was her! It was Lucy! Thank goodness for that!

Impulsively, he stepped towards his friend. But her expression stopped him. He bowed to cover his embarrassment. Of course, to Lucy he was a stranger. He should know that by now! She never remembered him from one world to the next. So this must be a new world after all, not the family from Old Wardour living in London.

For a moment, he saw in his mind's eye her face as they'd said goodbye last time. She'd been upset that they wouldn't meet again. And now here he was. Yet for her, it was all new.

Lucy's mother bowed her head and Lucy curtsied. The pale grey bodice she wore stopped her from bending, but her red skirt still swept the floor beneath her apron. Dark ringlets of hair crept out at the sides of her white cap.

"This is Joseph Hopkins," William said. "And this is Ellen," he gestured to his wife, "and Lucy. And I should have introduced myself. I'm William Lucas."

Joe tried not to smile too broadly. How astonished they would be to know that he knew them already!

He bowed to Ellen. "Call me Joe, please, madam," he said. "I'm delighted to make your acquaintance. And you too, Lucy." He beamed at her.

The girl smiled shyly, taken aback by the warmth of his greeting.

"I was on my way back from the wharf," William said, "when I found two rough men pressing him for the ships."

"But he looks younger than me!" Peter objected from the doorway behind them.

William nodded. "He is. And that means you should take care on your way to and from school. You know, there's barely a young man to be seen in the streets, and no watermen. It's almost impossible to get a boat. They're all afraid of being taken. It's a sorry state of affairs."

"What were you doing, Joe," asked Lucy's mother, "before my husband found you?"

"I'd only just arrived in London," he answered.

"Where from?"

Joe thought quickly. William Lucas had said something about plague in the east of the country. "Norwich," he answered, hoping this was reasonable.

"His family is dead. Contagion," put in William.

Joe lowered his head in a show of sorrow.

"Poor thing," murmured Ellen.

"You're not carrying it, are you?" Lucy sounded worried.

Joe shook his head. "I don't believe so."

"Don't be afraid, my love," her father said. "I wouldn't have brought him here if I thought he was. But there's no way he could have walked so far if he was ill. How long did it take you, Joe? Six days? Seven?"

"Seven," Joe said, grateful that he hadn't had to guess.

"What brought you to London?" Peter asked. "I thought Norwich was quite a big town."

Joe turned, thinking how to answer. "I couldn't bear to stay," he improvised. "All our friends and neighbours are being taken ill." The belief in Peter's face encouraged him to continue. "I couldn't watch them die too. I wanted to make a fresh start, away from all the memories."

There was a short silence.

Then Ellen said, "You must be tired and hungry. We'll have a good dinner shortly. It's actually another Fast Day here for the plague, but I'm afraid we don't always observe them, so you're in luck."

Joe was about to ask why they would fast for the plague, but stopped himself. Maybe it was a way of raising money, like a sponsored famine or something.

Ellen slipped her needle into the embroidery she was working on and rose from her chair.

"Lucy and I will help Mary and Elizabeth finish getting the dinner on the table. You sit down and rest. Peter and Solomon can keep you entertained."

Joe sat down in the chair she indicated. Peter went to the window. At once, the monkey sprang up the curtains and stalked along the rail with the poise of a tightrope walker.

William followed his wife and daughter out of the room.

"Is it fun, having a monkey?" Joe asked Peter. He found he was really glad to see Lucy's closest brother again. It made being here feel much more normal, especially after what he'd feared.

"It is, as long as he likes you." Peter grinned. "He can be mean if he doesn't."

"How do you know if he likes you?" Joe asked, thinking of the monkey's tail wrapped around his throat. Was it possible to be throttled by an animal so much smaller than you?

"Oh, you'd know alright if he didn't. He'd start by pulling your hair and pinching you, then move on to biting. My father has an apprentice who Solomon hates. He's the son of one of my father's distant cousins. The cousin and his wife both died of the plague, so my father took the boy in and arranged for him to be bound to the Worshipful Company of Mercers. But there's no sign of gratitude from him."

"Is that why Solomon hates him, because he's ungrateful?" Joe asked with a smile.

Peter laughed. "Maybe. As my father said, he's a very intelligent animal. Or maybe he just senses that Tobias is a rotten apple."

The smile froze on Joe's lips. "Tobias?" he said faintly.

"That's right," Peter said. "In fact, that was him, just passing the window. You'll meet him in a moment."

3

Joe groaned inwardly. Of course! Tobias! He'd been bound to be here. It would be so lovely to be in Lucy's world one day without him! But he was always somewhere in the background. And every time, he seemed to take an instant dislike to Joe.

The front door opened. Up on the curtain rail, the monkey sat completely still, alert.

"Solomon," said Peter, in a warning voice. But already the monkey had leapt down from the rail and scampered out of the room.

The next moment, there was a shout from the passage. "Get off me! You filthy little beast! Get off!"

Peter looked towards the door but didn't move.

"Is he attacking Tobias?" Joe asked.

Lucy's brother nodded.

"If you knew he was going to do that, why didn't you catch him before Tobias came into the house?"

Peter's eyes danced. "Solomon just expresses what the rest of us feel. If we're going to be stuck with

Tobias for seven years, we may as well have some fun out of it!"

There was another yell from the passage. "That is disgusting! Urgh! Why do you always do that?" And then really loudly, "Peter!"

Lucy's brother shrugged. "I suppose I'd better go and help."

"What has Solomon done?"

"He's just pooed on Tobias! He always does. I swear he waits! But he'll get nasty in a minute if I don't go and get him."

He left the room. Joe stayed in his chair. Tempting though it was to go and have a look, he knew that the longer he could escape Tobias' notice, the easier it would be to stay in Lucy's world.

A moment later, Lucy put her head around the door. "It's dinner time. Would you like to come and wash your hands?"

Joe followed her out of the room and along the passage to the kitchen at the back of the house. It was clean and bright, with white walls, a scrubbed table, and flowers on the window sill. The back door and windows stood open, looking out onto a small garden. But it was still blazing hot from the fire that burned beneath a cauldron.

Ellen stood beside it, removing a chicken from a spit. "If this weather goes on much longer," she said, "we'll have to start taking things to the bakers to be cooked. The fire's too much on a day like today."

At one end of the kitchen, the fair-haired girl was scouring a cooking pot, apparently using sand. Joe remembered the man he'd seen earlier with the barrel.

Lucy showed Joe to a stone sink in the corner with a tap above it.

"You have running water!" Joe exclaimed.

At once, he was afraid he'd given himself away. Perhaps running water was normal in this new world.

But she glowed with pride. "I know!" she said. "We have a tank which is filled through the pipes three times a week." She put a bowl into the sink and turned on the tap. A stream of murky liquid came out. It smelled horrible, like a stagnant pond. Running water it might be, Joe thought, but not like at home.

Lucy dipped her hands in the water and picked up a hard, white block from the edge of the sink.

"Is that soap?" Joe was sure he'd never seen soap in any of her previous worlds.

She nodded. "It's from Castile." Again she sounded proud. "My father brings it back from Antwerp. Don't use too much, though," she whispered. "It's much more expensive than the black stuff."

Joe tried to imagine black soap. It didn't sound very likely to get anything clean. But given the colour and smell of the water, what Lucy thought of as clean might be quite different from what he expected.

Peter followed them into the kitchen and washed his hands too. Solomon was nowhere to be seen. He must be back on his leash, Joe supposed.

Lucy led the way out along the passageway and into a large room opposite the sitting room. The lower walls were panelled in wood, and there were brightly coloured tapestries above the panelling. Joe saw that a flap had been cut into one of them for the door. He pictured himself taking a pair of scissors to a tapestry in his own time. People would be horrified!

It was dim in this room after the brightness of the kitchen. These windows, like the ones in the sitting room, looked out on the street with its overhanging buildings. A long, oak table stood in the middle of the room, spread with dishes. William and Ellen were already seated at either end, and the woman who'd passed through the hall earlier stood filleting a fish.

Joe looked more closely. Wasn't this the woman who'd been cleaning the furs at Old Wardour? That was why she looked familiar! Ellen had mentioned someone called Mary, and this *was* Mary! He smiled inwardly. Maybe the girl, Elizabeth, had been a servant at Wardour too. He didn't remember her, but that didn't mean anything. There had been hundreds of servants there.

He wondered whether anyone else would turn up – Morley, the steward, for example, or Peekes, the gatekeeper. Or what about Lucy's uncle and aunt? If people other than Lucy's close family were going to start turning up from one world to the next, he would eventually know everyone he met. For the first time ever, he wondered how long he would be able to keep coming back into Lucy's worlds. He pushed the question away. Now wasn't the time to think about it.

Peter took his place beside Lucy, and Joe sat down on the other side of her. Mary sat opposite, leaving two empty chairs to either side. There was a fifth empty chair between Joe and Ellen, and a sixth between Peter and William.

Joe wondered why the family had such an enormous table. Then he realised: three of those chairs would have been for Matthew, Cecily and Anne. He felt abruptly sad to know that he wouldn't be seeing them this time, or ever again probably. He hadn't been nearly as close to them as he was to Lucy and even Peter, but they'd always been there, part of the fabric of Lucy's life. Meeting them in each new time had been reassuring.

Elizabeth came into the room and sat down beside Mary. She was followed by an older boy.

"All cleaned up, Tobias?" asked William, with just a shadow of a smile.

"Yes, sir." Tobias scowled as he took his seat to the left of Lucy's father.

Joe studied him covertly. His curly, dark hair was longer this time than it had been before, spilling onto his shoulders. He was more plainly dressed than Peter and William, with square cuffs and a flat white collar showing over his grey jacket. There was not a frill to be seen.

"Let's say Grace, then." Everyone folded their

hands. "Good Lord, bless us," said William, "and all thy gifts which we receive of thy bounteous liberality, through Jesus Christ our Lord."

"Amen," replied everyone.

Joe peeped sideways with his head still bowed. At Old Wardour, the Graces had been very long. But this seemed to be it.

"Let's eat," Ellen said, "before it gets cold." She drew the roast chicken towards her and began to carve it. "Joe, pass me your plate."

Joe handed her the metal dish that was in front of him. Although the chicken was not especially large, she gave him a generous amount of meat. "That's umble pie, there," she said, pointing to a pastry oblong in front of William.

Joe watched Lucy's father, wondering if he'd misheard. Had Ellen said 'humble' pie? William, he saw, didn't take any of the pastry. Nor did Tobias or Peter. Perhaps it wasn't edible. After Lucy had helped herself, Joe followed her example, using his spoon to put a little of the pie filling onto his plate. Whatever umble was, it didn't look very appetising.

He helped himself to some of each of the other dishes as well. Besides the chicken, there was another plate of meat, and two types of fish. There was something with potato, and another dish that seemed to be oranges, lemons and eggs. There were also two sweet dishes which the family ate together with the savoury ones. Just like Old Wardour, there were no forks on the table, so they ate with their fingers, using bread to soak up the sauce.

"You must be thirsty, Joe." Lucy's mother poured some liquid from a jug into Joe's cup.

"Thank you, madam," he said. From the smell, he knew it was going to be beer. He took a sip. At least it was less bitter than the beer had been in Jorvik. But how was it, he wondered, that in Tudor times at Old Wardour, they had progressed to drinking water, even though they hadn't had running water indoors? Here, there was a tap and a sink in the kitchen, but it was back to beer again.

While they ate, the family talked of this and that: news from the neighbourhood, a disagreement between two of William's colleagues, and a pie filled with live blackbirds which had been served to the Dutch ambassador.

"I heard it was snake pie," Peter said.

"Well, either way, the ambassador was not amused," William said. "He doesn't seem to share the King's sense of fun!"

Everyone except Tobias laughed.

"When I passed Whitehall this morning," William said, "there was a huge queue of people waiting for the King's Touch."

"I've heard it works better on a Fast Day," Ellen put in. "That's probably why there were so many." Seeing the blankness on Joe's face, she said, "You've not heard of this?"

He shook his head.

"If you're sick, you can go and be cured by the King. People come from far and wide. He cures thousands of people every year who are suffering from the King's Evil."

Joe weighed up whether or not to ask what the King's Evil was. He decided to risk it.

Ellen looked uncertainly at her husband.

"It's an affliction that takes many forms," William said vaguely. "A lot of people have sores, but there was one little girl who'd been blinded by it. The King cured her, just by touching her face."

Around the table, there were murmurs of admiration. Only Tobias was silent, his face stonier than ever.

There was a good deal of food left when everyone had eaten as much as they wanted. Joe wondered if Ellen always prepared enough for unexpected guests, or whether she was still in the habit of catering for a larger family.

He copied Lucy and the others, dipping his napkin in a cup of water and using it to clean his hands and then rub his teeth. It felt strange to do something as personal as cleaning his teeth at the table, but nobody else seemed at all embarrassed.

"Shall we say Grace," William said. Joe put down his napkin and bowed his head once more.

"The God of peace and love vouchsafe always to dwell with us, and thou, Lord, have mercy upon us.

Glory, honour and praise be to thee, God -"

This time, the Grace did go on and on. Joe let his thoughts drift. He felt impatient to speak to Lucy on her own, and frustrated at the thought that she would need time to get to know him again.

"- through our Lord Jesus Christ," William said at last.

"Amen," replied the family.

Joe looked up to see what came next. Tobias' head was still bent, his lips moving silently. Mary and Elizabeth began to clear the dishes, and Lucy and Ellen rose to help them while Peter and William remained at the table.

Joe hesitated. At home, Mum and Dad expected him and Sam to help clear up. But this looked like an old-fashioned male-female division. He stayed in his chair, hoping he was doing the right thing.

"What lessons do you have this afternoon?" William asked his son.

"More Greek grammar," Peter answered. "And then a general assembly – three of us will be chosen to declaim in Latin on the Book of Ecclesiastes." He made a face. "I just hope it's not me!"

Joe swallowed, praying he wouldn't have to go to school with Peter this time. He'd struggled enough with dictation when they'd had lessons together at Fishbourne. But at least, he'd understood what he had to do. Nothing he'd learned at home would help him with what Peter was doing now.

William nodded. "It'll be worth it in the end," he said to Peter. "Now, remember to take care as you walk back. Steer clear of any rough types."

"Yes, sir." Peter got up and left.

William turned to Joe. "If you'd like to stay with us for a while," he said, "I'll find out this afternoon whether I can arrange something to occupy you. Or do you have family elsewhere in the country?"

"No, sir. I'd like to stay, if that's okay. I mean, if that's alright," Joe corrected himself hastily. He'd looked up the word 'okay' last year, and nobody had used it before Victorian times, and that had been in America, not England. He didn't yet know what year it was here, but he was sure it would be wrong.

William looked at Joe thoughtfully. If he'd noticed Joe's slip of the tongue, he didn't comment. "Very good. I'll see what I can do. Tobias, are you ready?"

Wordlessly, Tobias followed William out into the hallway and picked up his hat. William put his wig and his own hat back on, and they left the house together.

Joe hovered in the hall, wondering what to do.

"Don't hope for too much," Ellen said, coming out of the kitchen and shepherding Joe through to the sitting room, where she sat down at her embroidery frame again. "My husband managed to arrange an apprenticeship for Tobias, but with the way that's turning out, the mercers might be reluctant to take his recommendation again."

"But I don't want an apprenticeship!" exclaimed Joe in alarm. Then, afraid that he sounded rude, he added, "I mean, I don't want him to go to a lot of trouble on my account. I don't know how long I'll be here." He wished she knew how true this was.

But Lucy's mother just smiled. "As far as I'm concerned," she said, "you can stay for as long as you like. It's too quiet around here these days, and Tobias hasn't done anything to improve that."

"He's mean and selfish," Lucy said, as she came into the room. "There are plenty who'd give anything to be able to afford an apprenticeship like that."

"Your husband won't pay out any money on my account, will he?" Joe said.

"No, don't worry about that," Ellen replied. "He's a life-long member of the Company of Mercers, like his father and grandfather before him. Anything he arranges will be done on goodwill. But Lucy's right. They're some of the most sought-after apprenticeships in the land. People pay up to a thousand pounds for one."

Joe saw shock on Lucy's face. Obviously, she'd known it was a prized position, but not the actual cost. He wondered how much money a thousand pounds here would be in his own world. A hundred thousand, maybe. He'd have to ask Dad.

"Why is Tobias not happy?" he asked.

"Because the mercers stand for everything he's

been brought up to hate." Ellen gestured to Joe to take a seat beside Lucy, who had picked up some sewing.

Joe wondered again what a mercer was. "What is it exactly that Tobias hates about the mercers?" he asked, hoping this question might answer the other.

"Tobias' parents were Puritans," Lucy said. "Didn't you realise from the way he dresses?"

"The plain collar and cuffs, you mean? But he was wearing grey," Joe said. "I thought they wore black."

Ellen frowned. "Maybe you've only known Puritans of high rank. It would be ostentatious for someone like Tobias to wear such an expensive colour."

Joe bit his lip. He'd fallen into a trap of his own making, preoccupied with trying to guess what a mercer was, and pleased with himself for remembering something about the Puritans.

Where had he got that idea from, about them wearing black? The Puritans had disapproved of anything that was fun, or any kind of decoration, he remembered. But it was more than that. Then he recalled a painting he'd seen of a Puritan family. They'd been all in black. Perhaps they'd been wearing their best clothes for the portrait. That made sense. Or perhaps they were rich. Now that he thought about it, he could see that you'd have to be rich to have your portrait painted.

"In any case," Ellen was saying, "his parents

taught him that luxury is a weakness. So you can imagine, the mercers are the last company he would want to work for, as silk traders."

Joe nodded. It was starting to fall into place now. Silk was obviously a luxury, so if a mercer was a silk merchant and Tobias was a Puritan, of course he would disapprove of the Company of Mercers, and of William Lucas too, no doubt. "Then why did he take the apprenticeship?"

"He had no choice," Lucy's mother said. "The plague turned London into a ghost town. Hundreds were dying every week, thousands even, at its height. People fled the city, or stayed indoors, either afraid to go out or locked up like us."

"You were locked up? For how long?"

"Almost three months in total, until four weeks after Cecily died -" Ellen broke off.

"That's how it was here," Lucy said quietly. "Once one member of a family died, they painted a red cross on the door, and the words 'God have mercy', so people knew to stay away. They posted a watchman outside too, day and night, to make sure nobody came out."

"How did you get food?" Joe asked, aghast.

"There were two kind families among the mercers," Lucy said. "They gave food to the watchman for us. But then one of those families left town, and the other was locked up like us."

"Four of my children died of the plague," Ellen

said. "Matthew, Cecily, Anne and Francis." She cleared her throat. "And we had so little to eat and drink that my milk dried up. So baby Thomas died of starvation."

There followed a long silence.

At length, Ellen said, "I was telling you about Tobias, wasn't I? His father's business failed, with London deserted. Tobias' parents died bankrupt, so Tobias had to give up his place at the Inns of Court. But he hasn't forgotten that he once had a very different future than the one ahead of him now."

"He should be glad he's got any future at all," Lucy said, jabbing at her sewing. "The world would be a dismal place if everyone moped around, thinking about what might have been. Life goes on, and the living have to go on with it, don't you think, Joe?"

Joe nodded mutely. He knew she was right. But he felt like a fraud agreeing with her. There was no way he would ever experience the kind of loss she'd known in this last year. She thought he understood. He cringed at the prospect of telling her he didn't. But even if he wanted to, there was nothing he could do to change the fact that he was just a visitor here.

He'd always known he was unbelievably lucky to share a few hours of her life in all these different worlds. But it struck him now that he was luckier still to be able to go home.

4

For a while, Lucy and her mother worked at their tasks. Joe watched them, wishing there was something he could do. He felt uneasy, sitting idle while they were busy.

Presently, Lucy looked up from her sewing and said, "I've been thinking, if my father is able to arrange something for Joe, he'll probably start tomorrow. After that, he won't have much free time. Could I take him out this afternoon and show him around the city?"

Her mother looked doubtful. "Your father thought Joe probably shouldn't go out again after what happened earlier. If those men caught him a second time, even the two of you together wouldn't be able to save him from being pressed."

"Don't you think he might be safer if we dressed him up a bit? His clothes look rather worn out. If we put him in some of Peter's old best clothes, he'd look quite a bit richer. Then, if we do see the men, they might not dare approach him."

Ellen considered this. "You may be right. Let's see what we can find."

Joe followed Lucy and her mother out into the hallway and up the stairs. It seemed to be quite a big house, he thought. Downstairs, there were the dining and sitting rooms, and then at the back, the kitchen, and another door opposite. Up here, oddly, there were five doors rather than four, as well as a second staircase up to the attics.

"That's the house of office, in there," Lucy whispered, pulling open a door that Ellen had passed.

Behind it was a tiny space with a narrow, wooden box just lower than waist height. On the floor beside it was a pile of little booklets printed with text. The top one seemed to have had several thin pages torn off the front.

"You know, the close-stool, if you need to …" Lucy looked meaningfully at Joe.

"Ah, yes." He pretended to understand. Then it dawned on him. The 'house of office' must be the toilet! The box was the loo and the booklets were being used as loo roll!

Ellen led the way into one of the bedrooms at the front of the house. Like the bedchambers at Old Wardour, it had a four-poster bed with heavy curtains all around it, though this time, the bed had a kind of domed roof made from crimson material like the curtains. There was a sprout of crimson feathers at the pinnacle.

Curtains hung at the windows too, where at Wardour, there had been shutters, and a rug was spread across the floor. Wall hangings covered the two side walls, in front of which stood a cabinet and a large chest of drawers.

"Right, let's have a look." Ellen opened one drawer and then another. "Ah yes. Here we are." She handed Lucy a shirt with a frill all the way down the front and then two long pieces of lace. Next she lifted out a dark blue velvet jacket and a matching pair of breeches, like a smarter version of the ones Joe was wearing. "You'll need fresh stockings as well," she said, "and there are some galloshios to go with the coat and breeches. It's silly, really, to have kept it all. I just couldn't bear to pass it on yet."

Lucy put her hand on her mother's shoulder. "You might have another child," she said.

Ellen shook her head. "It took four years for Francis to come along after Anne, and another four for baby Thomas. I'm not as young as I was. I shall have to content myself with you and Peter."

Joe's heart ached to hear the sadness in her voice. His own mother might only have him and Sam, but that had been her choice. She hadn't had five other children who'd died.

Ellen handed the coat and breeches to Joe and burrowed in the drawer again.

"Take these, Lucy." She held out a pair of white stockings and some shoes of midnight blue brocade.

"You can help Joe get changed in your chamber."

Joe followed Lucy into the room next door. Like the first bedroom, it looked out over the street, or to be more accurate, straight into the front bedroom of the house opposite. It was smaller, having had the closet partitioned off, but it was still about the same size as Joe's room at home. It was similarly decorated to the room they had just been in, except that a circular mirror in a gold frame hung over the fireplace on the back wall.

"We're very fortunate," Lucy said. "My father brings all sorts of beautiful things back from Antwerp." She saw him looking at the mirror. "That was my birthday present earlier this year."

She put down the shoes, and laid out the stockings and shirt on her own four-poster bed. Then she took the other clothes from Joe and spread them out too. She sat on the edge of the bed and looked at him expectantly.

Joe blushed. She was waiting for him to undress. He bent to take off his shoes, hoping there weren't any tricky fastenings on anything he was wearing. Last time Lucy had helped him with his clothes, she'd known already that he didn't come from her world. This time, he had to try not to give himself away.

The shoes came untied easily enough, and he undid the garters at the tops of his stockings without difficulty, before removing his coat.

When he began trying to unfasten the shirt,

however, Lucy asked, "Aren't you going to take off the falling bands first?"

Joe's fingers stopped moving. What were falling bands? He followed her gaze. She was looking at his throat. She must mean the strips of material that had hung over the front of his coat. He fumbled at the back of his neck.

"Here, let me help you." She stepped round behind him and deftly untied the tapes.

Joe unlaced the neck of the shirt. Suddenly, he remembered his St. Christopher. He peeped inside his shirt as he took it off, wondering how to keep the pendant hidden. But beneath the shirt was a linen undershirt. It seemed ridiculous to be wearing what amounted to a long-sleeved vest in such hot weather. But it was clearly the way things were done here.

Looking at the clothes Lucy had laid out on the bed, he judged he was meant to keep the undershirt on. That was good. The St. Christopher could stay tucked away out of sight.

Blushing again, he unbuttoned his breeches, hoping that the undershirt was long enough to keep him decent. To his relief, however, he found that unlike Tudor times, he was wearing long, linen undershorts.

"Here you are, then." Lucy held out Peter's shirt. Joe slipped it over his head and looked down at the frill.

"You do up the ties on the inside." She watched

him for about half a minute as he struggled with the strings, then said, "Shall I help you?"

"Yes, please." Joe gave a rueful grin. "I'm not used to these things," he said truthfully.

Lucy laughed. "It's much easier than what I wear." In seconds, she had fastened the shirt and tied the new lace falling bands. She handed him the breeches, which buttoned up at the waist, like the pair he had taken off.

"Are there points or something, to fix the shirt to the breeches?" he asked.

"Points?" Lucy put her head on one side. "I don't think so. You just tuck the shirt in loosely."

Joe felt annoyed with himself. He'd been trying to be too clever. Perhaps they didn't use points at all now. From the words they used, it was obviously coat and breeches here, rather than doublet and hose.

He picked up the stockings. They were fine and smooth, and spotlessly white.

"They're silk," Lucy said. "They're lovely aren't they? We keep those for best, so they haven't been worn much even though they belonged to Peter, and before that to Matthew." She sighed.

As Joe put them on and tied the garters again, he thought about Lucy's eldest brother. In the last world, Matthew had died after a hunting accident. As far as Joe had been able to work out when he got home, it had been blood poisoning that had killed him. But in this world, he'd died of the plague.

More confusingly, Lucy's little brother, Francis, also seemed to have died of the plague last year. That puzzled Joe. Francis had been dead two years when Joe first met Lucy at Fishbourne last summer. So he should have died three years ago, not last year. Yet from what Ellen said, he'd still been four years old when he died.

Joe felt a sudden stab of guilt. Here he was, trying to work out a time-slip rule to explain Francis' death, when it must have been awful for Lucy.

He turned his mind to the other question that had been nagging him. He was sure he should know what year it was. He was in no doubt now that last year's plague must have been the Great Plague. They'd learned a bit about it at school a couple of years ago. There had been that village that had cut itself off after the plague was brought to them on cloth from a London tailor. But he couldn't remember for the life of him what year that was.

Lucy was still silent as he put the shoes and coat on.

"Is this right?" he asked, when he'd done the coat up. "It seems quite short." He plucked at the expanse of shirt showing beneath it. This was how his other clothes had fitted, but he couldn't quite believe they were supposed to be like that.

"You look very fine." Lucy smiled. "Are the galloshios alright? Not too big?"

Joe followed her gaze down to the shoes. They

had heels but no backs, like a woman might wear in his own world if she was going somewhere smart for the evening. "I think I'll manage," he grinned, hoping he'd be able to walk on the cobbles in them.

"All you need is an elegant hat and you'll look quite the young gentleman, although your hair is rather short. Is that how they wear it in Norwich?" She looked abruptly worried. "You're not a Roundhead are you?"

"No." Joe wondered whether to make up a story about cutting his hair to keep the plague away, but thought better of it. "I've always had it like this," he said.

They went back downstairs together.

"My, my!" exclaimed Ellen, as he entered the room. "What a transformation! Lucy was right – I'm sure you'll be safe from the pressmen looking like that. They won't dare come near you! Lucy, fetch Peter's hat he wears for church. That should finish off the outfit nicely."

Joe took it from her and put it on. It was black, with a wide brim and a ruffle of ribbons on the hat band.

"Perfect!" Lucy cried.

"You must still take care while you're out," her mother said. "And I want you back by six. Did you not want to get changed as well, Lucy? Mary has probably finished with the dinner things, so she could help you."

Lucy untied her apron and inspected herself. The

grey bodice had full sleeves to just below the elbows, but it was stiff-looking where it came to a point at the front. Below it, there was a band of silvery lace down the middle of the red skirt. All of it looked to Joe like it was made of silk. This must be the advantage of being a mercer's daughter, having beautiful material for clothes. Even so, it didn't look very comfortable.

"My Sunday petticoat and bodice are the same colour," Lucy explained. "But it'll take ages to unlace this one and lace up the other. The chemise looks clean enough, doesn't it?" She examined the frills of her shirt which were showing below the sleeves of the bodice, and craned her neck down to look at the shoulders and collar.

"It's fine," said Ellen.

"Then I'll just change my coif." Lucy went to a mirror on the wall and unpinned her white cap. Beneath it, her hair was wound up into a bun on the back of her head with ringlets at the front. From a drawer in the table, she took out a larger white head-covering, and draped it over her hair, tying it beneath her chin. It was just a looser version of what she'd taken off, as far as Joe could tell.

Seeing his expression as she turned round, Lucy said, "Don't you think the hood is prettier?"

"I suppose so," Joe said. He didn't feel that he was the right person to judge fashion in Lucy's world. "You look very nice," he added, and then blushed furiously.

Lucy blushed too, and picked up a pair of white gloves from the drawer. She eased her hands into them. They buttoned up nearly to her elbows.

"Back by six, then," Ellen reminded them.

"Yes, madam." Lucy curtseyed to her mother, slipped on a pair of outer shoes in the hallway, and led Joe out of the house.

"What fun!" she said, clapping her hands, as soon as they were out on the street. "I'm hardly ever allowed to go out now, except when I go shopping with my mother or we all go to church."

"Why not?" Joe sprang back as a carriage clattered past. A gang of small boys trotted after it, throwing stones. It was hard to see why you would bother travelling like that through the city, he thought. None of the carriages he'd seen had gone any faster than walking pace. But perhaps the idea was to be noticed.

"There's nobody I can go with any more," Lucy said. "I used to be allowed to run errands with Cecily, or one of our other maids. But Elizabeth is too young and Mary's too busy."

"What about Peter?"

"He's at St. Paul's School every day except Sunday. Apart from dinner, he's out from six in the morning until nearly six at night. "

"Don't you go to school?" Joe asked, as they set off along the street.

Lucy glanced sideways at him. He realised this

was one of those questions he shouldn't have asked.

"We may seem rich to you," she said. "But we're not wealthy enough for me to have a tutor. I finished my schooling four years ago."

Joe frowned. "How old are you?"

"Eleven."

"That's what I thought, same as me. How old were you when you started, then?"

"Five."

"So you had two years at school?"

"That's normal, isn't it?" she said. "I can read well enough and write a little. And I do the household accounts with my mother, so I know how to manage money. What would be the point of going to school to learn Latin and Greek like Peter?"

Joe had to agree with her. It was hard to see what earthly use there was in what Peter was doing this afternoon.

"Next year," Lucy went on, "I'm going to start doing my father's accounts with him. My mother does them at the moment, but they both want me to learn. That seems much more useful."

Joe nodded.

They walked on together. Around them, the street was just as loud as it had been earlier.

"What's that crashing noise?" Joe asked.

"That's from the foundries on Lothbury," Lucy said. "It's only a couple of streets from here."

"And that shrill noise?"

"Oh, that's the dung-cart. The rakers and scavengers have been through already to collect the general rubbish." She pointed to the baskets Joe had noticed outside the houses earlier on. "But they're still doing the rounds with the dung-pots."

"They're collecting poo?" Joe asked, horrified.

"From everyone who doesn't have a house of office or a privy in the garden. They come every day except Sundays."

"What do they do with it?"

Lucy thought for a minute. "You know, I'm not sure. I know the rubbish is taken out and left on the roadside beyond the city gates, for empty carts to take on their way back to the country."

"Lucky them!"

Lucy shrugged. "I guess the poo ends up on the fields, maybe. Though some of it definitely ends up in the river."

Joe pulled a face. "So is that the awful smell?"

"The dungcart? No, I don't think so. There's a tannery on the next street, so there's a bit of a smell of wee and dog poo from there." She sniffed. "But mostly it's coming from that churchyard."

Joe looked where she gestured. It occurred to him now that he'd passed a huge number of churches with William earlier, more churches than he'd ever seen in one town in his own world. Now he thought about it, this smell had been in the air most of the time, but especially when they passed a churchyard.

"What is it though?" he asked, pulling a face.

Lucy's brows furrowed. "Bodies, of course," she said. "I thought you said lots of people were dying in Norwich."

"They are."

"Well then, that's what you get when the graveyards are piled high. They've covered the bodies with lime to make them rot down quicker, but it takes a while."

Joe didn't know what to say. Suddenly, he saw something that stopped him dead. He snatched at Lucy's sleeve. "What is that?"

On the ground in front of them, a trickle of dark liquid had seeped out beneath a gate. It ran between the cobbles like a stream flowing around rocks.

"It looks like blood to me," Lucy said calmly.

Just at that moment, there was a hideous scream from the yard behind the gates.

The hairs stood up on Joe's neck. "What is it, Lucy?" He clutched her arm. "What's happening in there? Someone's killing someone!"

5

Lucy pulled her arm away from Joe and covered her ears with her hands. "It's alright!" she shouted over her shoulder, as she hurried on. "It's just the sow gelder."

"The what? What's he doing?"

"Gelding sows!"

"What's that?" Joe asked, when they were far enough away to uncover their ears. Too late, he realised it was probably something he ought to know.

"Making it so the sows can't have piglets, of course." Lucy sounded baffled.

"Why's he doing it right in the middle of town?"

"Where else would he do it?" She looked at him. "That *was* a butcher's shop. There are probably a hundred pigs in the yard there, and they've got to be done."

Joe tried to imagine a hundred pigs. It hadn't looked like a very big yard. The animals must be jammed in.

"The gelder's doing the ones that came from the Stocks Market this morning," Lucy said. "You don't want the sows getting in pig if you're going to eat them, do you?"

Joe recognised her tone. She was starting to get suspicious about the things he didn't know.

He huffed air out through his nostrils, trying vainly to clear the foul cocktail of smells. Just like the turkeys, the yard of pigs had brought the stink of the country into the city. On top of the stench from the graveyards, it made him feel quite sick.

"Don't you have this sort of thing in Norwich?" Lucy asked.

"Norwich is *nothing* like this," Joe said, thinking of the market town he'd visited once, years ago.

"So you won't have anything like that either!"

Joe looked up cautiously, wondering if this was a trick. But Lucy was pointing to an imposing building with stone columns and arches, and statues peering down at passers-by. "What is it?" he asked, genuinely impressed.

"It's the Royal Exchange. My father does a lot of business in there. There's a big courtyard inside, with shops and drinking houses all around. Anyone who's anyone goes there."

"Is your father there now?"

"Quite likely, unless he's at the Mercers' Hall."

"Can we go in?"

She shook her head. "Children aren't allowed."

They went to walk on, but their way had been blocked by four men in purple livery setting down a sedan chair. A small African boy also wearing purple ran around to the side nearest them and stood to attention as the curtain was drawn back.

A lady in a sumptuous dress and a towering wig stepped out. Her face had been painted white with red cheeks. It looked brittle, like a mask. A crescent moon and a cluster of stars had been stencilled in black onto one cheekbone, and Joe could swear her eyebrows had been stuck on. They looked thicker than they ought to be, and weirdly furry.

Ignoring the boy and her four servants, the lady strutted to the entrance of the Royal Exchange with a spaniel wedged under her arm. The boy scurried in behind her.

"*He*'s going in," Joe muttered to Lucy. "He's younger than us."

"That's different," she whispered. She sounded awestruck. "That's Lady Elizabeth Howell. The boy is her slave. He goes everywhere with her."

The boy disappeared. The liveried servants picked up the empty sedan and carried it off.

Joe felt a twinge of envy at the richness of their uniforms, and at the slave boy being able to go where he and Lucy could not. But of course, it was Lady Elizabeth who lived in luxury, not her servants. Being a slave here was unlikely to be any better than being a slave in Roman times. It occurred to Joe that this was the first time he'd seen a black face in Lucy's world since Fishbourne. Did that mean that the slave trade had begun? He had no idea.

Lucy let out a sigh. "How amazing to see her!" she said dreamily. "I've heard so much about her!"

"I thought she looked pretty strange," Joe said. "What had she done to her eyebrows?"

"All the great ladies do that." The corners of Lucy's mouth twitched. "They get rid of their own eyebrows and stick on new ones made of mouse-skin." She wrinkled her nose. "It must be horrible, actually."

"What, chopping up mice? I'm sure it is!"

"No!" She laughed. "Getting rid of your own eyebrows. The hair remover is made with cat poo and vinegar!"

"Oh no!" Joe shuddered.

"Well, it's either that or puppy-dog water!"

"Made with puppies?" Joe could hardly believe his ears.

"That's right," Lucy said with relish. "Roast puppy-dog mixed with a pound of earthworms washed in white wine."

Joe remembered the hair dye at Fishbourne, made with leeches rotted in red wine. "I'm glad they included wine in the recipe," he said sarcastically. "That makes anything work!"

"Does it?" Lucy's face was a picture of innocence.

He shrugged. "I don't know. I don't think so."

They walked on without speaking for a few moments. Then Joe remembered something.

"You were just saying about hair remover," he said. "I saw a carriage with a bald coachman when I arrived earlier. Why wasn't he wearing a hat or at least a wig?"

Lucy's eyes lit up again. "What colour livery was he wearing? Was there a crest on the coach?"

"He was in red and black, I think, but I didn't notice a crest."

She looked disappointed. "Red and black are quite common," she said. "If you didn't see an insignia, we won't be able to work out who it was. They must be rich, though. Only really wealthy people have bald coachmen – it's a way of making sure everyone knows that somebody important is in the carriage."

Joe grinned. How funny that a bald driver might be the same in Lucy's world as a supercar in his own time!

On their left, they came to a large open area whose roof was held up by giant oak posts. A smell of fish lingered in the air.

"This is the Stocks Market," Lucy said.

Joe chuckled at his own misunderstanding. She'd mentioned the pigs coming from here earlier. But he'd been imagining the stock market in his own world, where traders in suits shouted at banks of screens.

A couple of women were haggling over some meat or fish, and there was one pen of cattle. But most of the stalls had closed for the day.

"What's that building over there?" Joe asked, looking at a grand Tudor house on their right.

"That's the General Letter Office," Lucy said. "Though my father says you shouldn't use it for anything private. They read everything that goes through."

Joe tried to imagine Royal Mail doing that. It would be so boring and pointless!

"Come on." Lucy tugged Joe's sleeve. "I want to show you the Mercers' Hall. It's just at the end of Poultry. That's the name of this street - chickens and geese used to be sold here, although it's mostly taverns now."

Joe held back a smile. Lucy must have decided he was stupid to feel she had to explain that. You couldn't fail to see that these houses were taverns. They were doing a roaring trade for a mid-afternoon, judging by the singing and lurching around of the people outside them.

A little further along, they came to a junction where several streets met. The road they were on broadened here, and there was another church and a handful of houses beyond, standing in the middle of the thoroughfare like a kind of island.

With so much more sky visible here than where they'd been walking before, Joe was struck by the grey cloud that hung in the air. Chimneys poked up from every roof, most of them belching smoke in spite of the heat. Nonetheless, people strolled in couples or small groups among the carriages and carts, apparently enjoying the summer weather.

In front of Joe and Lucy was a squat stone building with battlements. Quite a few market stalls had been set up nearby and there were a lot of people milling around.

"That's the Great Conduit," Lucy said, before Joe had even asked. "Quite a few of the trades draw their water from there, and people whose houses don't get water piped from the New River. It's where the water sellers get their water as well."

"Do people have to pay for it?"

"Oh yes," she said. Then, with less certainty, "At least, I think so. The trades do, anyway."

They walked on until they came to an astonishing wooden building.

"This is it, the Mercers' Hall," Lucy said. "Isn't it fabulous?"

Joe gazed up at it. "It's amazing!"

The columns which supported the building were carved like totem poles with extraordinary creatures and gargoyles, painted all sorts of bright colours. Between them were panels decorated with vivid geometric patterns, and thousands of glittering panes of glass made up the windows all along the front of every floor of the five storey building.

Joe couldn't remember ever seeing a building like it in his own time. But of course, that was because most wooden buildings from the past had either fallen down or burnt to the ground, especially in London because of the fire.

A pit opened up in his stomach. The Great Fire of London! They'd learnt about it at school, the way all the houses had been built of wood, and the fire had spread because they were so close together. He looked around anxiously. The place where they were standing now was fairly wide, but every other street had been narrow.

He tried to remember what else he'd learned. It had happened in 1666, he knew that for certain – there was the Battle of Hastings in 1066 and the Great Fire of London in 1666. And hadn't it followed the Great Plague the year before?

He gulped, and looked at the buildings nearby, to see if any of them had dates. But, of course, that wouldn't help. Most of these had probably been built over the last hundred years. Unless he could find one being built right now, with a stone saying 1666, he still couldn't be sure.

"Shall we carry on down Cheapside to St. Paul's?" Lucy asked.

"If you like." Joe was distracted.

"We don't have to if you'd rather not," she said. "It's half ruined, anyway. They're still arguing over the rebuilding."

Joe frowned. Hadn't St. Paul's had to be rebuilt after the Great Fire? If the fire hadn't happened yet, why did it need rebuilding already? Or had the fire already happened years ago?

But that was impossible! He was sure that after the fire, the roads had been made wider and the houses had been rebuilt in stone. They'd been ordered to be flat-fronted too, without the upper storeys sticking out, to stop something like that ever happening again. No, this was London before the fire, quite definitely.

"The spire of St. Paul's was struck by lightning a hundred years ago," Lucy was saying. "Charles the First had just finished repairing it when he was executed. After that, it was desecrated." Her voice dropped to a scandalised whisper. "Oliver Cromwell's men even stabled horses in there!"

"That's terrible," Joe said.

"You know what?" Lucy lit up with enthusiasm. "Let's go down to the river and find a boat. I can take you up the Thames, out of the city. I'll show you the Palaces of Whitehall and Westminster, and we'll go and see Oliver Cromwell's head!"

"His head?" Joe echoed.

"It's on a spike above Westminster Hall, along with the heads of Bradshaw and Ireton." Spotting Joe's incomprehension before he could cover it, she explained patiently, "When King Charles came back to the throne, he had the men who'd killed his father dug out of their tombs and hanged."

"But I thought he was dead?"

"Not King Charles the Second. It was his father

who was executed, Charles the First." Again, she looked at him, puzzled by his ignorance.

"So Charles the Second decided to hang men who were dead already?"

"They *were* traitors," Lucy said. "The King had to make an example of them. They'd been buried in Westminster Abbey like heroes! So he had their bodies dug up and hanged to make it plain that they were no better than common criminals."

Joe made a mental note to brush up on kings and queens of England when he got home. Listening to Lucy talking about Oliver Cromwell and two kings called Charles was like looking at pieces of a jigsaw without the picture. If only he knew his history! But the bits he knew best were the times where he'd met Lucy before. None of that was of any use to him now.

"Do the heads still look like heads?" he asked, fascinated. "I mean, do they still have skin and hair and things?"

"I haven't seen them in ages," Lucy said, "and of course they've been up there for over five years now. But last time I went, you could see the skulls quite clearly, with just a few wisps of black flesh." She shivered. "You know they usually soak the heads of traitors in brine before they put them up, to stop the birds from pecking their eyes out. But, of course, Cromwell's eyes were already gone by the time they dug him up."

"That's revolting!" Joe exclaimed.

"You don't you want to see him, then?" Lucy was crestfallen.

"Well -" Joe hesitated. He knew he *did* want to see it, but he didn't like to say so. His parents always told him and Sam off for ghoulishness if they commented on ambulances or car crashes. On the other hand, this was his chance to be the only person alive to have seen Oliver Cromwell's head on a pole. It was too good to miss!

"Let's go down to the river and see if we can find a boat first," he said. "Your father did say there weren't any."

"Alright!" She clapped her hands. "We'll go along here a bit, then down Bow Lane. If we cut through, I think it'll bring us out between Dowlers Dock and Queenhithe, but not too close to either."

"Why would it matter?"

"Because they might have docked some of the ships there that they're filling with pressed men. I don't want to lose you, after I persuaded my mother to let us go out!"

"If you lose me, I'm in trouble anyway," Joe said. "I've no idea where your house is!"

She paused. "You're right. I should have told you when we came out, just in case we get separated. It's on Threadneedle Street."

"What number is it?"

"Number?"

"You know, house number. I don't think I'd

recognise it."

Lucy looked mystified. "Houses don't have numbers, do they? Ours is the one with the golden pheasant sign."

"Oh, yes. I meant to ask you about that," Joe said. "Why does it have that? It's not a shop, is it?"

Still, she frowned. "Lots of houses have signs. I thought it was like that everywhere. They don't have to mean anything. I think my father liked the picture because you see it embroidered on Chinese silk sometimes. But really it's there to help people describe where they're going. I should think half the people in London know the house with the golden pheasant."

"But some of these signs must mean something?" Joe pointed up at the sign hanging high up on the wall of the building in front of them.

"Of course," Lucy said. "That row of coffins -"

"Don't tell me," he interrupted. "It's a coffin-maker! Yes, I'm not a complete idiot. And the bag of nails on the sign back there was for someone who makes nails."

"Not just nails. An ironmonger," Lucy corrected him.

"But I saw one earlier with an elephant on it," Joe said. "Clearly, that shop doesn't sell elephants!"

"No, ivory," she laughed. "It sells combs and things like that."

"Alright, then. What about that one over there, with the cupid and the flaming torch?"

"That's a glazier."

"How would I know that from the sign?" Joe grumbled.

"Because the coat of arms of the Worshipful Company of Glaziers and Painters of Glass has two cupids holding torches on it." She sounded smug.

"Oh. That's not very obvious, is it?"

"Maybe not," she conceded.

"And I saw another one with Adam and Eve," he said. "Do they sell snakes or apples?"

"Apples and other fruit. You're getting the hang of it." She smiled encouragingly at him, as though he was a small child.

Joe snorted. "What about the one I saw with a unicorn and a dragon, then? Or was that just a private house?"

"No, that was an apothecary. He makes remedies for illnesses."

"Not out of unicorn's horns, surely!"

Lucy nodded. "It has magical properties! Didn't you know?"

"But Lucy!" Joe cried in exasperation. "You were with me when we had to rescue a unicorn's horn, back in Viking times! Only it wasn't from a unicorn at all! Your father told you that. They don't exist!"

Lucy gaped at him. She stopped walking and backed away a little. "I don't know what you're talking about," she said. There was fear in her voice. "I've never met you before. And unicorns *do* exist!"

"They don't!"

"Yes, they do!"

Joe took a deep breath. "Never mind about unicorns, it's the rest of it that's more important. There's something I need to tell you. But before I do, just tell me, what date is it today?"

She pressed her lips together. "It's Wednesday the fourth of July," she replied warily.

"Yes, but what year?" As he asked, Joe remembered that in the last world, they'd used some other system for counting years. He hoped he would understand her answer.

"It's 1666," she said.

6

"Oh no!" Joe cried.

"What is it?" Lucy was alarmed. "What's the matter?"

Joe took a deep breath and plunged into his explanation. "I already know you, Lucy. I've met you before, and your parents and Peter. And Matthew, Cecily and Anne too, though I've never met Francis. He'd already died before I first met you."

Lucy stared at him. Her face had gone white. "What *are* you talking about? We haven't met before! I'd remember you! And even if I didn't, my mother or father would. But they didn't, did they, and nor did Peter."

"He wouldn't," Joe said with a sigh. "None of you would remember me. It was in a different life. Well, three different lives in fact."

She shook her head. "You're talking nonsense! For another thing, you just said you knew Matthew and my sisters, but not Francis. But Anne died first.

You couldn't have met her after Francis was dead!"

Joe swallowed. Everything was so muddled this time, it was going to be harder than ever to convince Lucy of the truth. "Well, that part doesn't matter," he said, abandoning it for now. "The important thing is that I'm not from this world at all."

She looked at him, utterly bewildered. It was so frustrating! For him, this was the fourth time they'd had this conversation.

"Norwich isn't that far away!" she objected. "I wouldn't call it another world! You should know – you walked here!"

"I didn't though," he said desperately. "I just appeared out of my own time. One moment I was at home, the next I was here."

"But my father said those men were about to drag you away to the ships!"

"They were. That part is true. But he guessed the rest, about my parents being dead, and me walking to London. *He* said the plague was still raging in the east. Norwich was the first town that came into my head." He looked uneasily at Lucy.

Her features had hardened. "You mean, you're not from there? Your parents aren't dead?"

Joe shook his head.

"So you lied," she said quietly. "You lied about who you are. You lied about why you're here." Her voice rose. "Are your parents still alive, then?"

Joe nodded guiltily.

"Where are they?" she cried, outraged.

Joe winced. "My dad's probably at home in his new house in Winchester. And my mum's over near the Tower of London. We'd just visited it." He pictured Mum, frozen mid-step on the pavement while he crouched down just behind her.

Lucy turned on her heel and marched away from him. Joe hurried after her. They were going down a side street now, and the buildings had closed in again. The gloom matched his mood.

For a couple of minutes, Lucy completely ignored him. Joe wondered if he should just let her go, and make his way back to the house without her. That wouldn't solve the problem, though, only put it off until she got back later. Moreover, Ellen would probably be angry with him for leaving Lucy alone.

Suddenly, Lucy asked, "How did you manage to visit the Tower?" Her tone was still sharp, but Joe could tell that her curiosity had got the better of her. "Did you see the animals?"

"In my time, it's different to here," he said. "You just buy a ticket and go in. The animals aren't there any more. They got moved to London Zoo, nearly two hundred years ago."

"What's a zoo? Two hundred years ago?"

"I mean, two hundred years before my time. In my world, you see, it's 2015."

"What's 2015?"

"The date. The year."

Lucy fell silent again. Joe's heart sank. He couldn't see a way to win her round.

"1666 is an unlucky year," she said after a while, as though he hadn't spoken. "Because all the Roman numerals are in order."

It was Joe's turn to look bemused.

Lucy stopped and picked up a broken cobble from the street. "Here." She scraped awkwardly on the beam of the house next to them. "M for a thousand, D for five hundred, C for one hundred, L for fifty, X for ten, and VI for six. That's all the numerals in order."

"That's clever," Joe admitted. "And it *is* an unlucky year. But it hasn't got anything to do with that! This is the year of the Great Fire of London."

"The Great Fire?"

To his amazement, she shook her head and started to laugh. "You really *are* a bit mad, aren't you! The Great Fire was in 1633. My father talks about it sometimes. It burned half the houses on London Bridge, and a lot of Thames Street."

Joe thought for a moment. "That's really strange," he said. "I've never heard of that fire. At school, we learn about the fire of 1666. Most of what's inside the city walls is going to burn down, including St. Paul's."

Lucy's eyes widened. "Are you sure?"

Joe guessed she was humouring him, but then she said, "Actually, there *have* been some other bad omens. There was an eclipse a couple of weeks ago, and another one a fortnight before that. Eclipses cause sickness and famine. So maybe you're right. Maybe there *will* be a fire."

Joe snorted.

"What?" Lucy narrowed her eyes.

"Nothing!" Joe said, quickly.

"If you're so clever, when will it happen?"

Joe grimaced. "I can't quite remember. September, I think."

"And how does it start?"

"In a baker's."

"Which one?"

He bit his lip. "I don't know."

"Well, a lot of use that is!" she exploded. "You pretend to be someone you're not. Then you say there's going to be a terrible fire. But you don't know enough for us to stop it happening!"

Joe hung his head. "I'm not sure we could anyway, even if I could remember the details. This happened before, when you were living in Roman times." He ploughed on, despite the look of disbelief on Lucy's face. "I found out that your father was going to be put to death by the emperor, and I told him. I hoped he might be able to do something to prevent it. But the history books didn't change back in my own time. As far as I know, he was still killed."

"But this is different!" Lucy said impatiently. She seemed to have decided to ignore everything he said about past lives. "This is a whole city! If it's as bad as you say, we have to try and stop it!"

They paused on the street for a moment as a crowd of men burst out of a doorway, arguing in a language Joe didn't understand.

"Flemish, I think," Lucy said, seeing him watching them.

"I just don't know what we can do," Joe said, as the men moved away up the street.

"It's obvious!" she said scornfully. "If you're from the future, as you say you are, you just go back to your own world and find out exactly where and when it will be. Then you come back and tell me."

"Maybe." Joe hesitated. "But I don't have much control over how I get home, or back here again either." He thought of the time at Old Wardour when he'd deliberately got knocked off his horse. It had worked, but it had been risky, and painful too. In a way, it had been the start of all the trouble as well. He didn't much like the thought of using that strategy again.

Then he remembered his St. Christopher. "I've got something I have to give you," he said, looking around to make sure they weren't being watched. He unfastened the catch and pulled the pendant out from behind his collar.

"Where were you hiding that?" Lucy asked. "I didn't see it when you got changed."

"It was beneath my undershirt. I wasn't ready to tell you who I was." He could see she still didn't believe his story.

"And why do I need it?" she asked, plainly humouring him this time.

"Because it's the key to me getting back here," he said. "If you think about me when you touch it, and I'm thinking about you at the same moment, that's what pulls me back into your world."

"Right." She sounded unconvinced, but she took the St. Christopher from him.

"Do you know what it is?" Joe asked.

"Of course! It's a St. Christopher medallion."

He grinned. "Finally!"

"What do you mean, finally?"

"Finally, I don't have to explain it to you!"

"Of course you don't!" She was irritated.

"Don't be like that!" Joe gave her a friendly nudge.

"Like what?"

"Uppity. Just make sure you keep it hidden from other people, especially Tobias. He took it from you before, and it was really hard to get it back."

"That doesn't really surprise me," she said, with a grin.

Joe laughed. At least he wasn't going to have to convince her this time that Tobias was evil!

He watched her tuck the St. Christopher away through a slit at the side of her skirt. "You're sure it won't fall out?" he said.

"I've put it in the pocket I'm wearing."

"You're 'wearing' a pocket?"

"Yes, tied around my waist, of course. Oh, never mind! You know, I don't believe any of what you've just told me. But it would explain all the weird questions you've been asking!"

They paused again as a pair of cattle were driven past. "Now then," she said, "we're going to come to Thames Street in a minute. We have to be careful down there. My father says it's always really busy. There'll be a lot of carts going to and from the wharves and warehouses, and there's all the ship-building and repairs. There might be press-men down there, and there are sure to be cutpurses and footpads."

"What are they?"

"Robbers, thieves." She lowered her voice. "We shouldn't be going there, actually. I just want to see it. I've never been. When we go out as a family, we always take a boat from Tower Wharf. Promise you won't tell my parents when we get back?"

Joe promised. He wasn't sure this sounded like a good idea.

A new smell filled his nostrils now, a swampy, watery smell.

"The tide must be in," Lucy said. "At least that'll make it easier, if we can find a boat."

Joe frowned. He couldn't remember the tide ever being out when he'd been in London. How could that be?

"Why is it easier?" he asked.

"Because when the tide's out, the boats have to wait at the end of the jetties, where the water is. I hate walking out to them! It's often horribly slippery. I'm terrified of falling in."

"Into the mud?"

"Yes, but it's not just mud. There's all the nasty stuff that's been slopped out from the city."

"Like what?" Joe knew he might regret asking, but somehow, he couldn't resist.

"Poo and wee, of course," Lucy said. "Animal guts, the stuff from the tanneries, and the dyers and soap makers. There are even sometimes bodies, or bits of them."

"Bits?" Joe was aghast.

"When criminals are hanged, drawn and quartered, their legs and arms are nailed up around the city for everyone to see. And the heads of traitors are put on poles on London Bridge. So bits do sometimes end up in the river and get washed up on the tide."

Joe gulped.

"Right." Lucy put a hand on his arm. "Stay close to me."

Together, they stepped out onto Thames Street.

Joe felt as though his eyes were on stalks. It was busy, just like she'd said it would be. But then everywhere was busy. Was this different, more threatening somehow? Or did it just feel like it because of what Lucy had said?

The road was still narrow but most of the

buildings were bigger than elsewhere, timber-framed warehouses with the occasional crooked little house crammed in. There were no carriages or coaches and few gentlemen on horseback. Nor were there many women or children, as far as Joe could see.

There were a lot of older men, however, most of them swarthy and dressed in rough work clothes. One went past pushing a handcart piled high with crates. Another two staggered under the weight of several very long planks which they carried between them. Behind them, came a boy with a savage looking saw.

Two carts were pulled up side by side further along, almost entirely blocking the street. There was a lot of shoving and cursing as people forced their way past, ducking in and out of the men who heaved boxes and sacks to and fro.

Joe eyed a couple of older boys slouching against a stack of barrels, and a small child clambering over the coils of rope that lay outside one of the warehouses. The faces of all three were dirty and their clothes were torn.

"I don't think we should stay here," he muttered to Lucy. "I know you thought smarter clothes might keep me safe. But round here, they make us a target, don't you think?"

She nodded. "I thought Thames Street was right on the river," she said. "I didn't realise we'd have to cut through again. Let's cross over and go down that street there."

Reluctantly, Joe followed her to the back of the crowd jostling to get past the carts. He was glad he wasn't carrying anything that could be stolen – no wallet, no watch or mobile phone. But he was still afraid someone might pull out a knife and have a try.

Within a few seconds, there were people behind them as well as in front. Joe glanced around nervously. He and Lucy were surrounded. The smell of sweat and tobacco was pungent. He could taste it on his tongue.

Shouting filled the air. The nearest cart began to move towards them, the wheels screeching against the cobbles. Behind Joe, the crowd sensed an opportunity and pushed forward. Joe let himself be carried along with it.

Suddenly, his ankle turned beneath him. He staggered and fell. Hard lumps of ground bruised him. He put up his arms against the forest of feet. In slow motion, he watched a dent in the rim of the cartwheel slide downwards as it rolled over, bearing down on him.

All around, there was shouting, grinding, clattering. His ears roared.

"Help!" he yelled. "Somebody help me!"

But nobody heard him. The wheel kept turning, turning. In a moment, he would be crushed. He scrabbled to get clear of it. But the forest of feet closed around him.

"Help! Lucy!"

The world rushed in. The roaring fell suddenly

silent.

There was nothing but hissing.

He opened his eyes. The cart had gone. The crowd had gone. He was lying on the pavement in his own world.

His heart pounded and he was panting. If ever he'd needed to be pulled out of danger, this had been the time!

Gradually, the rumble of cars and lorries reached his ears again. His heartbeat slowed. The usual sickness was welling up in his stomach. But his relief was so great, he didn't mind. In a few minutes, he would be fine again, able to get up and walk on, as though he hadn't nearly been run down and killed.

"Joe!" The voice was close to him, urgent. "Joe? Are you alright? Can you hear me?" It was his mother. She sounded worried.

He sighed inwardly. Maybe everything wasn't quite perfect after all.

7

"What's the matter?"

Joe turned his head.

His mother dropped to her knees beside him. "I thought you were just tying your shoelaces," she said.

Joe lay still, waiting for his head to stop spinning. He knew that the longer he lay here, the more she would worry. But if he moved, he would throw up and that would be even worse.

Mum's face swam in front of him.

"Is this what happens?" she was asking.

Joe didn't answer.

"You can hear me, can't you? Joe?"

He closed his eyes and nodded his head just enough to reply.

On the pavement beside him, people walked past. Then someone stopped.

"Is he alright?" asked a man's voice.

"I don't know," Mum said. "I really don't know!"

"Would you like me to call an ambulance?"

"No!" Joe made himself open his eyes. He had to stop Mum from getting in a tizz. The last thing he wanted was to spend the rest of the day in A&E. He rolled over and began to sit up, clamping his mouth shut, just in case. But the nausea was fading now and the dizziness had almost passed.

"I'm fine," he said. "Really, I'm okay."

"If you're sure," Mum said doubtfully.

The man looked embarrassed. "Sorry. None of my business. I just thought you looked worried. Londoners can be terrible for walking on by."

"It was kind of you to stop." Mum said. "Apparently, this has happened before. I've just never seen it." She squeezed Joe's shoulder. "Are you alright, Joe? Really?"

"Yes, Mum, honestly!" Joe was starting to feel embarrassed too. He wished the man *would* just walk on by.

"Well, okay then ..." The man lifted his bag back onto his shoulder. "Bye."

"Thank you!" Mum called after him. Her cheeks were flushed.

She helped Joe to his feet. "Shall we sit down on that bench over there for a while?"

Joe looked where she pointed. He knew it would be a good idea to rest. But he knew, too, that Mum would start fretting and asking questions.

"We were going to go and get some lunch at one of those cafés, weren't we?" he said. It felt like weeks ago they'd decided to do that. "Let's go and sit down there."

"Alright then, if you're sure."

They walked along to the pedestrian crossing together without speaking. Joe was still struggling with the shock of being jolted back into his own world. It was all glass and brick and metal, hard edges everywhere, the buildings huge and austere. Lucy's London had been so much more human somehow. In his head, he was still there with her in the chaos and the crowds. But every few seconds, he saw a flash of the cartwheel turning, and heard again the horse's hooves strike the cobbles.

He felt sick to think that he would have been crushed, almost certainly killed, if he hadn't been pulled back to safety. In the past, the time-slip had usually been triggered by Tobias. But although each time, Joe had been gripped by terror, at least there had been a chance that Tobias wouldn't actually do what he threatened. This time, there was no doubt about what would have happened next.

Joe's heart pounded while he stood beside Mum at the traffic lights, waiting to cross the road.

"Are you sure you're alright?" she asked. "You're still very pale."

Joe nodded. There was nothing he could say that would stop her worrying. He just had to try to act normally.

As they sat down in the café, he said, "I was

wondering, is there a museum or anything about the Great Fire of London? I can't remember much about it, but while we're here, in the right place, it might be interesting."

Mum laughed. "I don't know what's to be done with you!" she protested. "First, you're asking the guide all sorts of questions at the Tower. Then you're out cold on the ground. Then, five minutes after that, you're back on your historical hobby-horse again!"

Joe grinned, abashed but nonetheless glad that he'd diverted her attention.

"As it happens," she said, "I think we're only about five minutes walk from the Monument. I'm sure that commemorates the Great Fire."

"Really?" Excitement buzzed in Joe's stomach. What good luck, to have the chance to find out everything he wanted to know straight away! A moment ago, his limbs had felt weak and tired. Now, he felt a fresh burst of energy. "Does that mean it started near here?" he asked, trying to keep his voice level.

"It must have done, I suppose. Let's stroll along there after lunch."

To Joe, it seemed to take an eternity for their food to arrive. When it came, he ate his sandwich in double-quick time.

"I'm not going anywhere without a cup of coffee," Mum said. "Why don't you have a piece of cake while you wait for me?"

It took ages for her to finish her own sandwich, and Joe had wolfed down his cake before she'd even touched her coffee. He was surprised by how hungry he was, considering he'd eaten a big lunch with Lucy only a couple of hours ago.

At last, Mum was ready to go. Joe felt a spark of anticipation as they set off along the road.

On the other side of the junction, they were immediately on Lower Thames Street, he saw. Presumably, that was part of the same street he'd been on with Lucy earlier, when he'd disappeared. It was odd, considering how far he'd walked, first with her father, and then with her, to have landed up so near the place he'd started out.

Of course, it was unrecognisable now. Two lanes of traffic streamed past in each direction, and the road was lined with one faceless block of offices after another. Even the oldest buildings had stone façades from long after Lucy's time. Joe felt a twinge of sadness, even nostalgia, to think of her London, with all of its amazing bustle and variety, about to disappear forever. Lucy was right. They had to try and stop the fire, even though he was sure they couldn't possibly succeed.

The Monument, when they reached it, was a giant stone column surrounded by buildings, many of which were as tall as it was. It couldn't have been like that when it was first put up, Joe thought. It must have towered over the rest of the city, even after all the houses had been rebuilt.

"There you are," Mum said, pointing to a plaque on the wall. "Designed by Sir Christopher Wren, 'to commemorate the Great Fire of London which burned for three days consuming more than 13,000 houses and devastating 436 acres of the City.' Wow! It must have been an inferno!"

Joe looked around, trying to get his bearings. If this was the spot where the fire had started, he needed a way of remembering it that he could transfer to Lucy's world. The problem was, nothing that he could see had been there in her time. Of course not! Her buildings had all burnt to the ground!

The only one in both worlds was the Tower of London. He wondered if he could pace out the distance from here to there. But Mum would find that very strange.

There was the river, too. That probably hadn't changed much. Except, he remembered, that it had filled and emptied with the tide in Lucy's time, and it didn't any more, so something had obviously been done to it. In any case, it would be just as hard to work out which point along the river bank he was level with, especially with all these buildings in the way.

"It says here," Mum went on, "that the height of this monument is the same as the distance to the bakehouse on Pudding Lane where the fire started."

Joe nodded. That was much more useful.

"I'm sure the baker was called Farriner, or

something like that," mused Mum. "It doesn't mention him here, but I remember thinking when I came across it that he'd been named for his job. Farriner comes from 'farine', which is French for flour. It's like those Happy Families books you had when you were younger, remember? 'Mr Tick the Teacher', 'Mrs Plug the Plumber'."

Farriner on Pudding Lane, Joe muttered under his breath, trying to commit the information to memory. Out loud, he said, "Does it say anywhere exactly when the fire started?"

Mum rolled her eyes. "You're so like your dad, sometimes," she said, "always wanting to get right into the detail."

Joe smiled. Dad had never had such a practical reason to know something like this, unless he'd been in the habit of time-travelling himself.

Out of the blue, it struck Joe that perhaps Dad *had* time-travelled as a boy. Maybe that was why he was so into history. It was possible that something like that ran in the family after all. Dad had never mentioned it of course, but then Joe hadn't told anyone he did it either. Perhaps they were keeping the same secret.

He filed the thought away as an interesting idea to explore later. Just now, the important thing was to find out as much as he could about the fire.

They walked around the Monument to look at the next side.

"Here we are," Mum said. "Second of September, in the dead of night."

"So does that mean sometime after midnight on the day that was going to be the second of September?" Joe asked. "Or would it be late at night at the end of that day?"

"I would have thought it means after midnight on the day that was going to be the second," Mum said. Joe could tell from her tone that she was wondering why it mattered. "Look, eighty-nine churches were burned down," she said. "I'm amazed there *were* eighty-nine churches inside the city walls!"

I'm not, Joe thought. *There were churches everywhere.* But he said nothing.

"And this is fascinating – it says the fire was harmless to the lives of the citizens," Mum pointed to the text. "Fancy that! Thirteen thousand houses and eighty-nine churches, but hardly anyone was killed. Isn't that incredible?"

Joe nodded. He felt reassured. That meant that Lucy's life wasn't in danger, even if her house was.

They walked around to the third side of the Monument. Here, there were some railings, and behind them, a door.

"I'd forgotten it was open to the public to go up," Mum said. "Still, all those stairs – I'd rather not do that with you today. It would be a disaster if you fainted halfway up, or worse, at the top."

They tipped their heads back and looked up at

the balcony high in the sky above them.

"That's okay," Joe said. "I don't mind." The only reason to go to the top would be for the view. It wouldn't tell him anything else about the fire.

"Now then, shall we go to St. Paul's while we're in the city?" suggested Mum. "Or shall we hop on a bus over to the West End and go to Covent Garden and Trafalgar Square?"

Joe thought about it. Was it worth walking over towards St. Paul's? It might be interesting, if he could walk over the same ground he'd walked with Lucy. But he was unlikely to know if he did, since nothing would look the same. And the St. Paul's they would see wouldn't be the one she knew. Presumably, that had taken decades to rebuild after the fire. He supposed she might eventually see this one when she was grown up, if she lived long –

Before he could finish the thought, he heard hissing in his ears. He looked at Mum to see if she was hearing it too. But she was saying something about the National Gallery.

The hissing grew louder.

Oh, no! he thought. He must be about to slip through time again! After all, he *had* been thinking about Lucy, so it wasn't impossible.

He panicked. How would his body cope with this happening twice in one day? He'd only just recovered from earlier! He looked around wildly for something to grab on to, some way of preventing it.

Was there anything he could do to stop himself?

But it was too late. The next moment, he was back on Thames Street in Lucy's time. Mum was gone. The Monument wasn't there. The vast buildings of his own world were nowhere to be seen.

His breath came out in a rush. He'd been holding it, he realised, trying to keep still like a statue, as though that would help! But here he was, back on the spot where he'd fallen beneath the cart a couple of hours ago.

He was on his feet now, not lying on the ground. And in any case, the crowd had gone. So had the cart. It was night.

He looked around, still reeling at being pulled back here so soon. In fact, it wasn't quite night-time, because the sky wasn't completely dark. The air was still warm. It must be late evening.

Flares burned at intervals along the street, and couples and small groups sauntered along. Joe wondered if it was still the same day as before. It was entirely possible.

He looked down at himself. He was wearing Peter's smart clothes. He put his hand to his head. Peter's hat was still there. For a moment, he felt surprised that it hadn't come off when he'd slipped under the cart. Then he shook his head at himself. How ridiculous! That was the least surprising part of all this!

He began to walk along Thames Street, trying to remember where he and Lucy had come from. Retracing his steps wasn't the most direct way back to her house, he knew, but it was probably better than trying to guess where to go.

There was a lot of shouting coming from the direction of the river. When he came to the next street that led down to the water, he saw the glow of firelight flickering on the walls of the buildings.

Alarm crackled through him. Had the fire already started? Was he too late? It could easily be two months since he was last here.

He hurried towards the river. The people in this tiny side street seemed quite unconcerned. But of course, apart from himself and Lucy, there was nobody else in all of London who knew about the disaster that was about to befall them!

Joe reached the quayside and halted, confused. Here was the water, broad, black and foul-smelling, flowing along well below the quay. The masts and rigging of two huge ships were silhouetted against the sky just along from where he stood, while further out, flat-bottomed boats with sails hauled themselves slowly up and down the river. Among them, countless little rowing boats nipped in and out, some with canopies like gondolas, lit up by the candles on their sterns. People sang and called to each other, and oars creaked and splashed. But there was no sense of urgency.

Between Joe and the ships in the dock, a bonfire burned on the quay. Not far along the other way was another fire. He peered out across the water in the fading light. Beyond the chaos of the river traffic, he could see bonfires dotted all along the far bank.

People stood around, drinking, shouting and laughing. There was music on the air, the sound of drums, violins and pipes playing a dozen different tunes.

He wanted to laugh. This wasn't the start of the fire! This was an enormous party!

8

Just then, a man came out of a tavern with a fiddle and struck up a tune. Joe listened. How peculiar! Here he was, over three hundred years back in the past, and yet it was exactly the kind of music he'd heard at barn dances and country fairs in his own world.

Almost immediately, people began to dance, in a happy but disorganised way. One of the dancers was wearing a ridiculous hat with feathers sprouting out of it. Another, in a dress with a wide skirt, turned out to be a man. In the glow of the fire, Joe saw that his face had been powdered white, and there were red circles on his cheeks and a tiny black diamond on his temple, just like a pantomime dame. His wig wobbled this way and that as he clumped around the quayside. The onlookers whooped and clapped, and the man fluttered his eyelashes and blew kisses to them.

After watching for a few minutes, Joe made his way back to Thames Street. With luck, he might find some of the landmarks he'd passed with Lucy. If not, at least she'd told him the name of the road where she lived, so he could ask for directions.

Thames Street itself was fairly quiet after the merriment on the quay. But in the narrow streets that led off it, light spilled from open doorways as private parties spread onto the road. People leaned out of their windows, singing and joking, raising their glasses in toasts.

Joe made his way up one of these, skirting one bonfire and then another, weaving his way in and out of the revellers. Really, with all these flames so close to the buildings, it was a wonder that the Great Fire wouldn't start tonight!

Perhaps it would, he thought abruptly. Perhaps the history books were wrong, and it hadn't been a baker's shop. Or maybe it had been, but it had been the same night as this celebration, whatever it was. If fire broke out in several different places at once, that would account for the whole of London burning down.

"Excuse me." He touched the sleeve of a woman who stood watching some children careering around, clearly enjoying themselves every bit as much as the adults.

The woman turned.

"Could you tell me, what's the date today?" Joe asked.

"It's the fourteenth of August, of course."

Joe frowned. So it definitely wasn't the night of

the fire. He wasn't sure whether to be glad or disappointed. He felt both, somehow. Was it wrong, he wondered, to want to be here when the fire happened? Wasn't it the same as wanting to see Cromwell's head on a pole? Voyeuristic, Dad called it, wanting to see someone else's misfortune. Joe's shoulders hunched up on their own, as though his parents were there to tell him off.

He shook himself. This was daft. Nobody else need know what was going through his mind.

He watched a small girl hopping about in the firelight and thought about the woman's exact words: 'the fourteenth of August, of course,' as though Joe should know. People didn't usually say 'of course' if you asked them the date, so it must be significant. But it meant nothing to him.

"What is everyone celebrating?" he asked.

The woman looked astonished. "Beating the Dutch, of course!"

"What, today?"

"No!" She hooted with laughter. "On St. James' Day last month. But the King declared a public holiday for today." As she spoke, there was a distant volley of bangs. "That's another round of fireworks up at Whitehall," she said.

"Oh." Joe was none the wiser. "It *is* still 1666?" he asked, just to be sure.

"Of course!" The woman was staring at him now, as though he were mad.

Never mind, he thought, heading on up the street. He would never see her again, so it didn't matter what she thought of his questions. The chief thing was that the fire wasn't going to start tonight, so there was still a chance that he and Lucy could try to stop it, although … He counted the days on his fingers. It would be eighteen days till the first of September, nineteen until the fire.

He felt deflated. The longest he'd ever stayed in Lucy's world was six days, which had been one of the times he was at Fishbourne. Other than that, it was usually only a night or two, or even shorter, as it had been earlier today – well, today in his own world, which was about six weeks ago in Lucy's time.

He came to another crossroads with a slightly wider road. In both directions, there were more bonfires, more music and dancing, drinking and laughter. He didn't see any buildings he knew. He wasn't even sure he'd been along this street before.

Plucking up courage, he approached a man who leant in a doorway with a tankard of beer. "Excuse me, sir. Which way do I go for Threadneedle Street?"

The man pointed. "Take a left just along there, where Dowgate Hill meets Walbrook, and carry on up until you come to the Stocks Market. The street you want is off to your right as you cross Poultry."

Joe nodded and thanked him. He wasn't sure he quite understood, but if he could get as far as the Stocks Market, he should be able to find his way from there.

"Was the young gentleman looking for Threadneedle Street?" asked a man's voice behind Joe. "We're going there ourselves."

Joe turned around.

"We'll gladly take you with us," the man said.

Joe caught his breath. The man hadn't recognised him yet, but Joe knew quite well who he was. It was William Lucas, again! In a way, it was a stroke of luck. But he had no idea what to say!

Time stretched out as he gazed wordlessly up at Lucy's father. How was he going to explain why he hadn't returned with Lucy? The family had made him so welcome. At the very least, they would want to know where he'd been since then. He swallowed.

"Joe!" Lucy ran forward from William's side. "It *is* you, isn't it?" She caught hold of his hand. "How extraordinary! I was thinking of you only a few minutes ago!"

"Well, I never!" exclaimed Ellen.

"Master Hopkins, returned from the war!" William Lucas beamed and shook Joe's hand firmly.

"And he's even managed to keep the clothes we lent him in pristine condition!" Ellen shook her head in wonder. "I should never have let you and Lucy go out that afternoon," she said. "Are you well? You weren't wounded or mistreated?"

"It was my mistake," Lucy said quickly. "I was so sure we'd be alright with you dressed like that. But when those men grabbed you -" She shot Joe a look.

Joe was bewildered.

"I did try to find you," William said. "I went to Bridewell, and to Tower Wharf. But they denied all knowledge of you! They swore they'd never even taken a boy of your age."

"What was it like on the ship?" It was Peter who spoke now, his eyes round. "What kind of ship was it? Did you go into battle? Did you fight on St. James' Day? Were there cannons? And hand to hand combat? It must have been really exciting!"

"Enough, Peter!" William raised his hand. "Give the poor boy a chance to speak!"

"I'm fine, thank you," Joe said politely. Lucy must have told them he'd been taken by the press-men. At least they seemed to think that was a satisfactory explanation. As for all Peter's questions, it was very tempting to invent some brave deeds to impress him. But Joe didn't dare, certainly not in front of William and Ellen. The only book he'd read about sea-faring in the past was *Treasure Island*, and that was about pirates, not war. He was bound to get lots of things wrong if he made it up.

"It wasn't as exciting as you'd think," he said, hoping he sounded modest. "My ship didn't see much of the action. In fact, I spent most of my time scrubbing the lower decks." They nodded. "Anyway, I'm glad to be back, and in time to see some of the celebrations!"

"We've been across the river for a picnic in Lambeth fields," Lucy said, seizing the chance to turn the conversation in a different direction. "And then we went to the pleasure gardens at Foxhall."

"Yes, but Father wouldn't let us go to the bear garden!" Peter cast a look of mock resentment at William.

"The cockpit was quite violent enough, I thought," said Ellen with a grimace. "Honestly, Peter, you're a savage, wanting to watch these poor animals forced to fight! That little cockerel didn't stand a chance against the bigger one."

"I agree," Lucy said primly. "It was horrible!"

"Well, you seemed pretty fascinated!" teased Peter. "You didn't take your eyes off the birds!"

"Come now," said William. "Foxhall was supposed to be a pleasant family outing, not a source of dissent!" He put his hands on Lucy and Peter's shoulders. "I think we should get ourselves safely home, before we get caught up in the late-night revelry! It tends to get out of hand," he said to Joe, "especially the apprentices. I expect it's the same in Norwich. They get so few days off a year, it's not surprising they go a bit wild when they get an extra day's holiday. I should know! I was one once!" He grinned ruefully. "I hope you'll come home with us?"

"I'd love to," Joe said. "Thank you, sir!"

William steered them forward, around the crowds and up Walbrook. It was properly dark now, and the light of the fires flared. For a second, Joe thought of the flames soon to come. In less than a month, all this would be gone, unless he and Lucy could find a way to save the city. He shivered.

They passed the dark hulk of the Stocks Market and emerged onto Poultry, where the party was even more riotous. Beyond another bonfire, Joe spotted the General Letter Office, and a minute or two later, they passed the Royal Exchange where he and Lucy had seen the lady with her African slave-boy. It was odd to think that for Lucy, that afternoon was weeks ago, when it was so fresh in his mind.

"Here we are then," Ellen said, as they arrived outside the house. "Home to bed. Though I'm not sure any of us is going to get much sleep tonight, with all this noise outside." She opened the front door.

At once, there was a high-pitched screech.

"You remember Solomon?" Peter went down the dark hallway to the room opposite the kitchen and reappeared with the monkey on his shoulder.

Joe reached up to take his hat off. But before he could, the monkey made a leap and grabbed it by the ruffles, shaking it gleefully and then clamping the brim in its teeth while it scampered off to the sitting room.

"You need to train that animal!" Ellen said in exasperation. She went along to the kitchen and returned with a burning candle, with which she lit three more candles which stood ready on the hall table. "I'll see about finding you a nightshirt and cap," she said to Joe. "You don't mind sharing with Peter, do you?"

"Of course not," Joe said. "It's very kind of you to have me."

There was a creaking of floorboards upstairs, and the sound of a door shutting.

"That'll be stay-at-home Tobias," William said. "I invited him to come to Foxhall with us, but he declined. I don't think he went out with the other apprentices either. Such an odd boy! Still, at least we'll get a decent day's work out of him tomorrow while the rest are nursing their sore heads."

Ellen and Lucy started up the stairs. Their flickering candles made their shadows jump around on the walls. Behind them, without a candle of his own, Joe had to feel his way. The stairs were uneven, and twice, he nearly tripped. That would be another way a house might catch fire, he thought, if you fell down the stairs carrying a candle, or stumbled and set fire to a wall-hanging. People at home loved to talk about 'a disaster waiting to happen', but this place really was one!

Ellen led the way into Peter's room and lit another candle on top of the chest of drawers. The bed was another four-poster with heavy curtains and a domed roof just like the others. Like Lucy's room, you would hardly guess that this belonged to a boy rather than an adult. The only toys here were a box of wooden bricks and a small, carved wooden horse and rider.

There was a pair of stockings hanging over the edge of the chest of drawers, but no other clothes to be seen. Joe guessed that clothes were too expensive for people to have many, so they looked after them better. He was sure that was how it had been in every world so far, though nobody had ever actually told him so. Clearly, books weren't common yet either, and as for plastic, that wasn't going to be invented for centuries.

Joe thought of his own room, strewn with clothes, books, Lego, and all sorts of other toys. People had so much stuff in the modern world – well, people like him, anyway.

He waited for Ellen to pull out a spare mattress from beneath Peter's bed, but she went to the drawers and took out a long linen shirt and a brimless cap like the one William had worn last time Joe was here. This cap was plainer, with embroidery in a strip around the edge. But Joe couldn't help thinking he would look rather girly in it.

"Peter will show you where we keep the tooth powder and cloths if you want to clean your teeth. But I imagine you don't mind waiting until the morning!" Ellen smiled.

Joe shook his head.

"You know where the close-stool is, don't you? We don't have chamber pots in the bedrooms. And Mary will bring up a bowl of water in the morning for you both to wash."

Joe nodded.

"Alright then, we'll bid you goodnight."

She picked up her candle and left the room.

Lucy hesitated, waiting for her mother to be out of earshot. But before she or Joe could say anything, Peter came in.

She shrugged. "Goodnight," she said. "You know where we are if you need anything. Peter's a heavy sleeper. I hope he doesn't keep you awake with his snoring!" She jabbed her brother in the ribs and went out, taking her candle with her.

Joe grinned. "You can't be worse than my brother," he said to Peter.

"You have a brother? I thought your family was dead."

Joe coloured. "They are. He is." He wanted to kick himself. He'd spoken much too cheerfully for someone who'd lost his whole family in the last couple of months. He sat down on the edge of the bed with his back to Peter, and began to undress.

For ages, he lay rigidly beside Lucy's brother, waiting for him to go to sleep. He hated sharing a bed with someone else, but once Ellen had gone, he'd realised that this was what she'd meant by 'sharing with Peter'.

The room was terribly hot. From beyond the curtains, shouts and laughter carried on the night air through the open window. Still, the bed was big and the mattress was softer and more comfortable than any of the mattresses he'd slept on in Lucy's other worlds, even if it did smell of sheep's wool.

At last, Peter began to snore. Very quietly, Joe pushed back the sheet and got out of bed. He hoped Lucy wasn't asleep already. He needed to tell her where and when the real fire was going to break out so that even if he wasn't there to help her, she could still try and do something to stop it.

At the door, he paused to listen, then cautiously turned the handle. At that moment, the door of the room opposite opened. Joe shrank back.

There was a rustle as someone crept along the hallway and down the stairs. Silently, Joe opened the door of Peter's room and tiptoed onto the landing. He peered down into the darkness. It was Tobias. He was going out.

On instinct, Joe ran to grab his clothes. As he scrambled into them, he hoped Peter really was a heavy sleeper. It wouldn't be good if he woke up and found Joe gone.

But whatever Tobias was doing at this time of night, wherever he was going, Joe felt certain he was up to no good. Talking to Lucy about the fire would have to wait. For now, he had to follow Tobias.

9

From the hall downstairs came the sound of the bolts being shot across as Tobias unlocked the front door. There was a screech from the monkey tethered in the back room, and a muffled curse. Then Tobias went out, closing the door behind him.

Joe crept down the stairs, still pulling his coat on. He would have to get back before Tobias if he was going to avoid being locked out. But that was a problem for later.

"What are you doing?" hissed a voice.

Joe jumped.

At the top of the stairs behind him, he could see the pale shape of Lucy's nightdress.

"Tobias has just gone out," he whispered back. "I think he might be up to something. I was going to follow him."

"Wait for me! I want to come!"

"Alright. But hurry, or we'll lose him. I'll wait for you outside."

Joe turned the door handle. Again, there was a scream from the monkey. Joe winced, expecting Lucy's parents to come out to see what the noise was about. But nothing happened. He slid out onto the street and pulled the door almost closed behind him, leaving it open just a crack for Lucy.

The number of people out here had dwindled since earlier, but the noise had not. The shouting was louder, the singing more raucous, and the party had a wilder edge to it.

Joe looked up and down the road for Tobias. Had he delayed too long, talking to Lucy?

Then he saw a shadowy figure dart across the street down to the right, the same way he'd gone out with Lucy. In the flickering light of the fires, he couldn't be sure it was Tobias. Yet, the furtive way the person was moving seemed at odds with everyone else. This wasn't someone enjoying the celebrations. This was somebody doing something secret.

Keeping under the cover of the buildings where they jettied out over the street, Joe hurried after him. Parts of the road were now completely dark, where households had shut themselves up to go to bed. But at the crossroads ahead a large bonfire was still blazing. The smell of rotting bodies from the churchyards was as pungent as before, but the smell of smoke was stronger than anything else.

At the crossroads, Joe paused. He thought Tobias had slipped down the street to the left but he couldn't see him. He blinked and frowned. Surely he hadn't been that far behind. Then two people emerged from a doorway just a couple of houses down.

Joe pressed himself against the wall and looked back towards Lucy's house. A small figure stood on the street. Joe waved. Lucy raised her hand and hurried towards him, lifting her cumbersome skirts.

While he waited for her to catch him up, Joe turned back to watch Tobias, afraid of losing him again. But the other boy had relaxed his pace now and walked with his companion as though they were out for an evening stroll together.

"It's so busy and so bright tonight," Lucy said, as she reached Joe. "My father doesn't like us being out after nightfall because of footpads. We sometimes are in the winter of course, because the sun sets so early. But then the streets are dark and almost empty."

"Maybe that's why Tobias chose tonight for whatever he's doing," Joe said. "With all the celebrations, it won't seem strange to anyone that he should be out."

"What makes you so sure he's doing something he shouldn't?"

Joe looked at her. "What time is it?"

"I don't know. Around midnight, I think, maybe later."

"And is it normal to go out at that time?"

"No, of course not. But it's hardly a normal night!"

"That's true," Joe admitted. "But your father seemed to think Tobias had been at home while everyone else was out enjoying themselves. That's quite weird, don't you think?"

"I suppose so."

Ahead of them, Tobias and his companion hesitated for a few moments. Joe and Lucy waited in the shadows.

"What do you think he's doing, then?" Lucy asked in a low voice.

"I don't know," Joe said. "But you remember I told you I'd met you before?"

She nodded. "I didn't believe you, not about any of it, until I saw you vanish from under that cart! I was glad I could say you'd been pressed for the ships. I don't know how I could have explained it otherwise. But I was still in a lot of trouble, especially with my mother. I think she felt bad for letting us go out."

"Oh, Lucy!" Joe sighed. "I'm sorry. It's so unfair! That's happened before. I disappear, and you get punished. Try and blame me next time. Or maybe," he brightened, "you might be able to blame Tobias. I told you, didn't I, that Tobias was there before, in all the other worlds. Well, every time, he was scheming to get his hands on something that wasn't his, or trying to get ahead somehow."

"Was he actually bad," Lucy asked, "or just unhappy or mistaken? I mean, we all want to get the best for ourselves, don't we?"

Joe made a face. "Perhaps he was unhappy. But I've never seen him smile or laugh except when he was being cruel. Every time, he was prepared to use you or hurt you, if it got him what he wanted."

"Me?" Lucy looked alarmed. "Why me? I have almost nothing to do with him. I hardly even have cause to speak to him! It's obvious that he disapproves of our family, but why would he pick me out?"

"I don't know. Maybe he won't this time." But Joe knew he didn't really believe it. "Hang on a minute! Where's he gone?"

They scanned the street ahead.

"We have to be careful," Lucy muttered. "If he and his friend went into one of these houses to collect somebody else, we could be right outside the door when they come out."

"Wait!" Joe touched her arm. "Is that them?" Three shadows emerged from a house and turned left along a wider road. "Do you have any idea where they're going?"

"That's Lombard Street," Lucy said. "It becomes Fenchurch Street."

"What's along there?"

"I've no idea."

Silently, they followed Tobias and his two companions along the road, keeping at a careful distance. Suddenly, the three figures disappeared between some buildings.

"Where have they gone now?" Joe cried.

"There's an alleyway there, I think," Lucy said softly. "I don't know where it comes out. Maybe behind the Pewterers' Hall."

"The what?"

"The Pewterers' Hall. The pewterers are the craftsmen who make and work pewter – you know, the grey metal that's used for cups and plates."

"Why would they be going there?"

"No idea. Maybe one of the others is apprenticed to them. It's more than likely they're all apprentices, if they're the same sort of age as Tobias. Or maybe they're just cutting through to somewhere else, though I don't know where."

They waited a few more seconds, to be sure they weren't too close behind the three boys, and then hurried to the mouth of the alleyway.

It was pitch dark between the buildings, except for a faint light at the far end.

"We should have brought a lantern," Lucy whispered.

"I'm not so sure," Joe replied. "At least, Tobias won't be able to see us."

Together, they began to feel their way, Lucy with her skirts hitched up, Joe following on tiptoe, acutely conscious of the white silk of the stockings he'd been lent. The alley was so narrow that two people would barely have been able to pass one another, and the ground was heaped with stinking muck and rubbish. Joe tried not to breathe in. He couldn't see where he was putting his feet, and it was horrible, feeling his shoe sink into something soft, or squelch through something wet.

Lucy stopped abruptly. In the blackness, Joe fell into her.

"What is it?" he breathed, getting his balance and trying to see over her shoulder.

She shifted to one side so that he could stand beside her. "I think you were right," she murmured. "It looks like a secret meeting of some sort."

Just a few metres in front of where Lucy and Joe were hidden, six boys huddled together, talking in whispers, glancing over their shoulders now and then.

One of them had put a lantern down in the centre of the circle. There was no other light here, no glow from the city's bonfires, and no windows in any of the buildings that backed onto this tiny yard. The lamp shone upwards, making the boys' faces look like skulls. Their shadows loomed on the walls around them like an army of monsters coming out of the darkness.

Joe looked upwards. One of the walls was very high, like the end wall of a church. That must be the Pewterers' Hall. There were houses or workshops the rest of the way round, and a second alleyway on the far side of the group. But no street led to this spot. If you didn't know it was here, you'd be unlikely to stumble across it. That must be why Tobias had chosen it.

Somehow, Joe felt sure it *was* Tobias who had chosen the place. He was taller than all but one of his companions, so he might well be older than them. But in any case, Joe couldn't imagine him letting anyone else take the lead.

Tobias was standing with his back to Joe and Lucy. Joe could just make out his voice among the rest, though the words were indistinct. Gradually, however, all six boys began to drop their guard, and speak normally.

Suddenly, Tobias' voice rose clearly above the others. "Why not tonight?" he pressed them. "If we all agree that we should do it, why delay?"

"It's too dangerous!" objected one of the boys. "There are too many people about. One of us is bound to get caught."

"Not necessarily," Tobias said. "And with all the fires burning already, nobody will ever know how it started. Don't you see? Tonight would be perfect! God's punishment on the city for all this debauched behaviour! You've seen it: the drinking, the revelry, the godless pleasure!"

Joe shuddered at the hatred in the other boy's voice.

"Even my own master squandered the day the Lord gave him, eating, drinking and making merry with his family!" Tobias raised his fist. His arm was shaking. "God shall smite them all!"

Joe heard Lucy draw breath sharply. He turned

his head. Her face was taut with outrage.

"That's us!" she mouthed.

He nodded.

"I say we rain brimstone and fire upon the city," Tobias hectored, "as was 'rained upon Sodom and upon Gomorrah brimstone and fire from the Lord out of heaven.'"

Joe guessed he was quoting from the Bible. He sounded like a lunatic preacher.

Tobias looked around the group. "And I say we do it now, tonight! William Malkin and John Dodgson to the Tower, John Archer and Thomas Foreman to the Palace of Westminster, and myself and William Freeman to the Palace of Whitehall."

Lucy stiffened. "Oh, my God!" she breathed. "They're going to kill the King!"

"Are you sure?" Joe whispered.

"He lives in the Palace of Whitehall."

"What's at Westminster?"

"The government."

"And at the Tower?"

"I'm not sure. It's a royal fortress, but I don't know who or what's inside."

Joe tugged her sleeve to draw her further back into the alleyway. "Listen to me, Lucy," he said in a low voice. "You don't need to worry. It's the fourteenth of August today, isn't it?"

She nodded.

"Then it won't happen. There's nothing that

happens until the Great Fire of London, and that's not till the second of September. It's going to start at Farriner's bakehouse in Pudding Lane, in the early hours of the morning. That's where we need to be."

She frowned. "I don't see how you can be so certain."

"Of course I'm certain! History says that's what happens!"

"But does history say what *doesn't* happen because somebody stopped it?" she retorted. "What about the plots that get discovered? The plans that are foiled? What if the only reason Tobias fails in this is that somebody finds out? That somebody could be us, now, overhearing him! We have to do something!" She moved along the alley, to listen again.

Joe felt his stomach sink. What if Lucy was right? What she was saying made sense. Maybe fate had brought them here to stop Tobias. Perhaps they couldn't just trust to history that he wouldn't carry out his plans.

"We shouldn't rush into anything," one of the boys was saying. "I thought we were meeting to talk about possibilities."

There was a murmur of assent from the others.

"Very well," Tobias said savagely. "Since not one of you is brave enough to carry out the Lord's will tonight, we'll meet here again tomorrow. I shall bring the plans with me. The Lord has instructed me in every last detail of our task. You'll see how we shall set the fires that will cleanse this country of its wicked rulers, and blow half of London into the sky as a punishment!"

Lucy gasped. "So that's what's at the Tower! Gunpowder!" In her fright, she spoke louder than she'd meant to.

Tobias froze. "What was that?" He whirled round. "There's someone listening!"

The other boys looked stricken.

"Thomas, John, search the alleyway over there!" Tobias barked. "You two, check those dark corners!"

Lucy didn't move. She seemed to be rooted to the spot. The fifth boy was coming straight towards her.

Joe grabbed her. "You mustn't get caught!" he hissed. "Go, quick! Run back and find Tobias' plans and hide them! I'll delay him as much as I can."

He pushed her back along the alley, and heard her stumble and slip as she fought her way through to the street beyond. Before he could turn back towards Tobias, he felt a hand on his collar.

"He's here!" called the boy.

Joe kicked and struggled, not really to stop the boy hauling him out, but to cover the noise of Lucy escaping.

"Out of the way, you weakling!" A second pair of hands grabbed Joe's shoulders. Tobias pushed the other boy aside.

A moment later, Joe was slammed against the

wall of the Pewterers' Hall. His head spun. His hat was on the ground. Tobias' hand was at his throat, choking him. Joe looked into the familiar face of his enemy.

"Who are you?" snarled Tobias. With the lamp on the ground, his eyes were in shadow. But the twist of his mouth was as unpleasant as ever. "How much did you hear?"

Joe spluttered. At least Tobias didn't recognise him from the meal he'd eaten with Lucy's family. That meant he wouldn't connect him to Lucy.

Joe's gaze flicked past Tobias' shoulder. The five other boys had melted away.

"In fact, don't bother to answer," snapped Tobias. "It makes no difference how much you say you've heard! I can't risk it. Either you come with us and help, or I'll have to kill you. Which is it going to be?"

10

Joe clawed at Tobias' hand where it was locked around his throat. He couldn't breathe.

Tobias loosened his grip, but didn't let go.

Joe gulped for air. "Us?" he got out, between gasps. "Who's us?"

Tobias glanced round, then looked again more carefully, peering into the shadows.

"Let them burn in hell!" he thundered. "Run off like whimpering dogs, every last one of them! And all because of you!" He thrust his face close to Joe's. His breath was sour. "You'll have to help me now!"

Joe tried to think what to do. These moments with Tobias almost always propelled him back into his own world. But he didn't want to go home yet! He wanted more time with Lucy. And he didn't want to have to explain to her parents next time why he'd disappeared from their house in the middle of the night. If only he could find a way of deflecting the older boy so it didn't happen.

Tobias gave Joe a shake. "Do I take it from your silence that you're ready to do the Lord's work? Or would you rather die, here and now?"

Joe opened his mouth to speak. "Die?" he said, playing for time. Suddenly, he had a crazy idea. "I can't die," he said, trying to make his voice sweet. "To die, I would first have to live. But I'm not mortal like you."

He felt pleased with himself. 'Mortal' was exactly the right word, especially talking to somebody like Tobias. Mortal was the word they used in the Bible for being human rather than an angel or a spirit or something.

He watched hesitation flicker across Tobias' face. "Not mortal?" the other boy said, suspiciously. "Then what are you? Your flesh feels solid enough. You look like the rest of us." All the same, he let go of Joe.

Joe cleared his throat, determined to seem calm although his heart was racing. This was a risky plan.

"I'm God's messenger," he said. "An angel, if you like. Your guardian angel."

Tobias narrowed his eyes. "Is that so?" he growled.

Joe held the other boy's gaze. His lips were dry but he didn't dare wet them. Maybe this wasn't going to work. It was a pretty long shot, after all.

"God has sent me to show you the way, His way," he said. "He doesn't want you to burn palaces or blow up the Tower. Don't you remember what happened to Guy Fawkes?"

Tobias spat on the ground. "Filthy Catholic traitor! Don't liken me to him!"

"He thought he was doing God's work, too," Joe persisted. "Whatever you think, he believed he was acting in God's name." He warmed to his idea. "You know, God sent an angel to stop Guy Fawkes, just like He's sent me to stop you. But Guy Fawkes didn't listen. Don't make his mistake!"

Tobias gave a high-pitched laugh. "Fawkes was in league with the devil, like the rest of his sort! Ours is the true way. And the Lord has made *me* His instrument! 'For it is written, vengeance is mine. I will repay, saith the Lord.'" Tobias' eyes glittered. "I've heard God's voice, telling me what to do. And if I die doing it, I'll be remembered as a martyr, not a criminal like Fawkes!"

Joe watched Tobias steadily. The older boy sounded mad. And yet, Joe didn't feel afraid now. He must already have won Lucy enough time to get away. And though if Tobias tried to hurt him, he would still disappear, that might actually be a good thing. It might make Tobias believe he really was an angel.

"No," he said coolly. "You're wrong."

"How dare you deny the Lord?" Tobias shrieked. He grabbed Joe's arm and twisted it behind his back, as he'd done once before. "You're just trying to save your own skin! But it's blasphemy, that's what it is!"

He sprang round behind Joe. "You know what," he snarled in Joe's ear, "*you* can be the one that does the deed. That way, *you'll* be the one with blood on his hands. *You'll* be the one who'll be hanged, drawn and quartered for it. Because *you* will get caught. I'll make sure that you do!"

He shoved Joe forward, giving his arm another wrench. Something cracked in Joe's wrist. Pain swirled in his head. He felt dizzy and sick. Any moment now he would hear the hissing in his ears, he told himself. He just had to hold on till it came.

But there was nothing, only distant shouting and singing, the faint crackle of the bonfires, his own stumbling steps, and Tobias' curses as he forced Joe back into the alleyway.

In spite of himself, Joe began to panic. Tobias obviously didn't believe he was an angel. And whatever pain he was inflicting on Joe now, there would be much worse to come. Why hadn't he been pulled back into his own world? What if it didn't happen? What if it failed this time?

His mind leapt ahead. Tobias might force him to do something terrible, like set fire to a building. He could refuse – he *would* refuse. But if Tobias put a burning torch in Joe's hand, he could make Joe move it about as he liked. Joe would be little more than a puppet, unless he fought back.

Concentrating as hard as he could, he blocked out the pain in his wrist and arm. What he was about to do might break his bones, if they weren't broken already. The thought horrified him. But it was his only chance.

With the next step, he kicked his foot hard backwards, driving it into Tobias' shin. Before the other boy could react, he flung his body forward and down, as though he was going to throw his opponent over his head. There was a dull, slumping sound, though whether it was him or Tobias landing on something in the alley, he didn't know. His shoulder snapped. A burning sensation shot through his neck and down his arm.

Silence fell, soft and black, all around him.

As he surfaced from the darkness, his first clear thought was that he really ought to take up judo or karate. It would be good to know how to defend himself properly against Tobias.

He opened his eyes. He was lying on the pavement on his side. It was daylight.

Mum's feet were in front of him. Beyond, he saw two other pairs of feet. He closed his eyes quickly. If he pretended to be unconscious, there would be time for the nausea to pass before he had to get up.

He wondered if he'd dislocated his wrist or shoulder. The pain had been like fire. It didn't seem to hurt now, but until he moved, he wouldn't know for certain. He prayed that he hadn't broken anything. What a stupid thing he'd done! When Jackie Chan threw the baddie over his head in films, he knew what he was doing. Joe snorted.

Instantly, his mother dropped down beside him.

"Can you hear me, Joe?" She sounded horribly anxious.

When he didn't answer, she turned to one of the people standing nearby. "Is he going to choke?" She was panicking. "He won't swallow his tongue, will he?"

"He should be safe," replied a voice. "He's in the recovery position. Look, here comes the ambulance."

Joe groaned.

"Are you back with us?" Mum asked. "The paramedics will be here in a moment. You're going to be okay."

Okay, Joe thought, apart from the fact that he'd wrecked their special day by collapsing not once but twice. The worst of it was, he didn't feel up to carrying on with it now anyway. So they'd be wasting another afternoon waiting around in another hospital. He felt tears prickle behind his eyelids.

At St. Thomas', Joe lay on a trolley in the corridor of A&E for two hours. Mum hovered beside him, nervous at first, and then more and more frustrated. All the while, doctors and nurses ran frantically to and fro, dealing with patients who were much worse off than Joe.

Finally, when he was sure he was feeling better, he persuaded Mum that they should leave. "I expect I just need to eat something," he said.

"But you'd had a sandwich and a piece of cake just before you fainted."

"Yes, but I was still hungry," he lied. "And I'm starving now!"

He climbed down from the trolley, feeling like a naughty boy climbing out of the window at school.

"I'm afraid Joe's discharging himself," Mum said to a nurse hurrying past.

The nurse bit her lip. "I'm so sorry you haven't been seen yet!" she said. "I'll do my best to make sure someone gets to you soon, if you wait a little longer."

Joe shook his head. "Don't worry," he said. "I don't want to be a bother to you. I feel fine now."

As they stood on the steps outside the hospital, he and Mum looked at each other and began to laugh.

"I feel so guilty," she said. "I should have made you stay!"

"What would be the point?" Joe said. "We both know we could have waited another two hours, just for someone to check me over and tell me I could go!"

She nodded. "All the same, let's get something to eat from somewhere else. I'm sure there are plenty of cafés in the hospital, but I'd be looking over my shoulder all the time, waiting to be told off!"

Joe grinned.

"So where are we now?" he asked as they walked out of the gates. "Where is St. Thomas' Hospital?"

"On the south bank of the Thames," Mum said, "next to Lambeth Palace, on the other side of the river from Big Ben and the Palace of Westminster."

The Palace of Westminster, thought Joe. *That's one of the buildings Tobias wants to burn down.* Immediately, he shut the thought out of his mind. He really, really didn't want to wind up back there again. Twice in one day was more than enough!

It was a couple of days before he dared to let himself think about Lucy at all. He wondered if she'd got home quickly enough to find Tobias' plans, and if so, what she'd done with them. He was sure Tobias wouldn't manage to carry out his threats. But was that because he'd frightened him off? Or had Lucy stopped him? There was no way of knowing.

And then of course there was the Great Fire itself. In Lucy's world, it had been just over two weeks away. Would he be able to get back in time to see it? Maybe there wasn't any point, since he was sure he wouldn't be able to stop it. But it would be a shame to miss it when he'd been so close.

As the first week passed, and then the second, Joe began to feel tense. He knew quite well that there was no relationship between the speed time passed at in Lucy's world and in his own: six weeks had gone by for her between his first and second visits to Threadneedle Street, when for him it had been less than two hours. Equally, in Jorvik, it had once been over a fortnight in his time, but only two days for her. Still, it felt as though it must be getting close to the time of the fire.

At least, he'd managed to tell her where and when it was going to start. But then he worried whether she would remember, and if she'd understood what he'd meant by 'the early hours'. What if she thought he meant early in the morning? She might get there to find the fire already blazing. Or if she did get the time right, she might get hurt trying to put it out.

It was maddening to feel so helpless. He had to do something! But the only thing he could think of was to find out more about the fire.

So after school on Thursday, he went to the library.

"You're not starting another project now, are you?" the librarian said when she saw him. "It's nearly the summer holidays. Or is this another of your historical crazes? What period is it this time?"

"The Great Fire of London," Joe said, ignoring her raised eyebrow. It was starting to annoy him that people thought he was faddish.

"Ah, the Restoration," she said.

"Restoration?"

"The period after Charles the Second was restored to the throne."

Seeing Joe's confusion, she went to a shelf and took a book down. "This will give you the background. But in a nutshell, it's this: after the Tudors

– Henrys Seven and Eight, Edward, Mary and Elizabeth – came the Stewarts. We had James the First – the target of the Gunpowder Plot – followed by his son, Charles the First, who was an irresponsible and foolish king."

Joe tried to remember what Lucy had said about him. He was sure she'd mentioned him.

"Charles had a habit of agreeing to everything people asked," the librarian went on, "even when he was secretly doing the opposite. It's no wonder the country fell into civil war."

Joe frowned. Dad had talked about the English Civil War. "Was that the Cavaliers and the Roundheads?" he asked.

"That's right. The King's side were nicknamed the Cavaliers, and Oliver Cromwell and the Parliamentarians were the Roundheads. They wanted to get rid of the monarchy altogether."

Joe suddenly remembered Lucy asking if he was a Roundhead because his hair was short. She'd looked worried, he recalled. Presumably then, her family were supporters of the King. And hadn't Oliver Cromwell been a Puritan, like Tobias? That must be another reason why Tobias hated Lucy's family so much, not only because William was a mercer. It made more sense now.

"The English Civil War went on for nearly ten years, on and off," said the librarian. "But eventually, the Roundheads won. Oliver Cromwell was one of the men who signed Charles the First's death warrant."

"Oh yes!" Joe exclaimed. "That was why the next King had Cromwell dug up and his head put on a pole, wasn't it?" The things Lucy had told him were falling into place now. He felt a stab of regret that he hadn't got to see Cromwell's head after all. Perhaps they might go and look at it next time, whenever that was.

The librarian smiled. "That's right. When Charles the First was executed," she said, "his son, Charles the Second, escaped to France. Famously, he hid in an oak tree to avoid being caught. While he was away, Oliver Cromwell defeated the last of the Cavaliers and ruled over England as Lord Protector until he died.

"After that his son took over, but he was weak and useless. So Charles the Second returned from France in 1660, and voilà! You have the Restoration!" She made a gesture with her hands like a magician producing doves from a hat.

What a peculiar woman, Joe thought.

"I've always thought the Restoration period would have been quite fun," she was saying, "if you exclude the Plague and the Fire."

Joe blinked. Those were pretty big events to exclude! "Why's that?" he asked.

"It was time of pleasure," the librarian said. "Charles the Second was nicknamed the Merry Monarch, you know. If you really want to get a feel for what life was like then, you should read Samuel Pepys' diary. It's all on the internet. Fascinating stuff!"

Joe thanked her, and took away a stack of books. He knew she was just trying to be helpful, suggesting the diary. But he couldn't see how it would tell him much he didn't already know.

On the way home, he found himself mulling over what she'd said about it being a time of pleasure. That was what had made Tobias so furious, people enjoying themselves! That was what he wanted to punish. In a way, Joe thought, it was like religious extremists in his own world, hating the West for being decadent. And like the terrorists on the news, Tobias was determined to do something about it, even if that meant dying himself.

For a second, Joe's blood seemed to stop moving. How had he not recognised the parallel? He'd been distracted by the fact that Lucy's world was a different time. Yet Tobias' intentions were the same! He was planning to kill the King, burn down parliament, and blow up half of London. That was nothing short of an all-out terrorist attack!

Cold crept over Joe's skin. He'd never expected to actually meet a terrorist. But that was what Tobias was this time, a religious fanatic hell-bent on punishing his enemies. And worst of all, he was living in the same house as Lucy.

Fear flared inside Joe. He'd felt brave for spinning out those minutes behind the Pewterers' Hall with Tobias, even though it meant physical pain. He'd been glad to gain Lucy some time so she could run home and search for Tobias' plans. Yet he'd known all along that he wouldn't have to face the consequences.

How had he not seen that he was leaving his dearest friend to prevent a terrorist attack on her own? He'd abandoned her to face a danger even greater than the Great Fire itself! What if Tobias had got back to the house and caught her? Even if he hadn't, he might still suspect she knew.

What if she hadn't managed to find the plans? Then she would have followed Tobias when he went out again in the night. Only this time, she would have been alone.

Joe longed to get back into Lucy's time more than ever before. He thought about her as often as possible, and wished there was something else he could do to make it happen. Sitting on his bed at home, he took out a pencil and paper and tried to draw her. Without a photograph to copy, the picture wasn't very good. But it was something he could carry in his pocket.

In the meantime, he hoped fiercely that she wasn't in any danger. *And please, please, please,* he thought, *let her think of me again soon.*

11

The last few days of the school year went by in a bit of blur for Joe. It was the end of his time at Colborough Junior, and on the last day, his classmates wore white T-shirts which they asked each other to write on.

"Didn't you want to join in?" asked his friend, Matthew, when he arrived wearing a blue and green top.

"I forgot," Joe said. It was true. But he also felt too old for all this. He didn't really see the point either. It was hardly a big goodbye: most of his class were going on to the same secondary school, and the younger children would be coming up behind them. The only people they were leaving behind for good were the teachers, and Joe wasn't sure he would ever want to wear a T-shirt with all their signatures.

Even worse, some of the girls in his class were going round with books for people to write messages in. Two girls Joe didn't really like came up to him and asked him to write something. He cringed. They seemed so young and silly compared to Lucy. And what did they expect him to put? He hadn't said anything more significant to either of them over the last four years than, "Could you move up a bit?" or "Pass me that pen, please"!

Above all, he resented the interruption to thinking about Lucy. So on the first day of the summer holidays, he sat down with his library books to do some proper thinking about her.

"You're weird!" said Sam, when he saw what Joe was reading.

Joe ignored him. His brother couldn't possibly understand. But as far as Joe was concerned, it was time well spent. Even if he couldn't trigger the time slip, it was still good to be prepared, just in case.

There wasn't much in the books, however, that he hadn't already found out at the Monument, or seen for himself with Lucy. He did discover that 'pudding' was an old word for guts and bowels. So Pudding Lane had been named after the bits of animal intestines that fell off the butchers' carts going down to the dung boats on the river. It wasn't quite the row of bakeries and cake shops Joe had imagined!

The other new fact, which gave him comfort, was that only six people had died in the fire. That meant that Lucy was almost certainly safe, assuming she avoided trouble with Tobias. It also meant that if he managed to get back there to see the fire, he shouldn't be in danger himself.

When he wasn't wishing he could make it happen, Joe was worrying about when it would be. It was infuriating that it was so unpredictable! There were moments in his own time which would have been perfect, when he strained his ears to hear the telltale hissing. And there were awkward moments, when he was glad to stay put.

When it did finally happen, it was definitely one of the awkward times. And although he'd been waiting for it for over three weeks, the time slip still took him completely by surprise.

He was at the swimming pool with his brother, and had just dived into the water. Everything was muffled, so he didn't notice a hissing sound. There wasn't the dizziness either, presumably because he wasn't upright.

The main reason he was surprised, though, was that he hadn't been thinking about Lucy, or at least not the Lucy he'd met most recently. He'd been remembering swimming with Petrus at Fishbourne, and trying to recall whether Lucy had been able to swim in that world.

As he plunged through the water, thinking about this, he found himself suddenly dry, dressed, and standing on firm ground.

The dizziness caught up with him then. He stretched out his hands to either side. His fingers brushed against rough plaster. He blinked a couple of times and took a deep breath. The stink nearly made him retch. He shut his mouth quickly.

This must be the alleyway behind the Pewterers' Hall, he thought. He checked over his shoulder, just in case Tobias was still there, but there was no-one to be seen.

As he picked his way back to the street, he wondered what time it was. It must be day, because he could make out some of what was on the ground beneath his feet: fish heads and chicken carcasses, heaps of muck that had to be poo of some kind, a puddle of greasy, grey liquid, and a pile of mouldy vegetables rotted away into slush. Yet even though he could see all this, it was not a bright day. The thread of sky visible between the buildings overhead was dark grey, as though a storm was about break.

Then he noticed the noises coming from beyond the alleyway. Louder than anything else was the snapping of fire. In fact, that was louder than he'd ever heard it before. There was a lot of shouting and wailing too, over the rumble of cartwheels and the clash of hooves. From some way ahead of Joe came a crash of something large falling, like a tree being felled.

At the end of the alley, he emerged into a street which was thick with smoke. It tasted acrid on his tongue, and dry, as though it was sucking the moisture out of him.

A cart rocked towards him, its load towering above the carter's head. The horse's ears were flat back and Joe could see the whites of its eyes. Poor creature, he thought. It was terrified.

All around, people were running to and fro. Many of them were clutching armfuls of belongings which they dumped down on the ground. Outside the house nearest the alleyway, a trembling boy helped a man stack crates and boxes higher and higher. Joe couldn't see any flames from where he stood, but from the rattling carried on the wind, the fire couldn't be more than a street or two away.

It seemed to be in the other direction from Lucy's house, as far as he could tell. He ought to set off back along Fenchurch Street right now, and go straight to her house. But somehow, the pull of the fire was irresistible. Like a moth drawn to a flame, he turned left down a side-street towards it.

This street was even more crowded and noisy than the last. People barged past each other cursing, many of them staggering under the weight of their haphazard loads. A woman dragged two large baskets along, stopping every few paces to shove the bed covers and wall hangings back in where they had tumbled out. Another rushed around in circles shrieking. Her arms were draped with tapestry curtains which she was trying vainly to keep out of the gutter.

A young woman with a hugely pregnant stomach stood beside a cauldron filled with pottery dishes and cups. As a cart approached, she ran forward and pleaded with the carter to take her and her cauldron. But the wheels just ground remorselessly onwards.

Joe came to a crossroads. Out of the shelter of the buildings, the wind was strong, driving the heat of the fire ahead of it like a desert storm. Giant flakes of ash and sparks the size of leaves blew towards him.

He flung up his hands to shield his face. His palm burned as a cinder brushed against it. His eyes were really watering now and there was a bitter taste in his mouth. He knew he should turn back. Instead, he made his way on, down a road to the right, magnetised by the fire.

People were stampeding past him now. Among the crowd, Joe noticed three boys pushing overloaded handcarts, urged on by a gentleman who was shouting at everyone to get out of the way. Several rough youths appeared from a side-street, rolling barrels in front of them. They looked about them shiftily, as though they expected to be stopped. At one house Joe passed, the front door opened and a grubby man sidled out. Beneath his arm were two large packages, and Joe saw him pat the bulging pockets of his coat as he hurried away.

Suddenly, the sky burst orange. The snapping noise surged to a roar. A box flew out of an upstairs window ahead of Joe, followed by two pictures and a rolled up rug. In the street beneath, a boy retrieved them and stuffed them onto a cart already piled high.

"That'll be a guinea a mile out to Kensington," the carter said.

"But that's twenty times the usual price!" cried the man beside him. "Where will I find four guineas?"

"I can get my boy to start unloading," threatened the carter, with a hard glint in his eye.

"No, no!" The man wrung his hands. "We'll pay! We'll pay!"

Joe was appalled. In a few minutes, this man's house would be gone. But the carter was determined to profit from his misfortune.

"At least you *can* pay," wailed a woman from across the street. "Some of us can only take what we can carry."

Joe eyed the grubby-looking baby in her arms, and the gaggle of dirty-faced children hanging on her skirts. She wouldn't be able to take much more than them with her, he guessed.

The crackling was louder than ever now. Joe peered through the smoke. There, beyond the heads of the crowd, were leaping flames.

He caught his breath, stunned by the enormity of the fire that loomed over everything. Sparks were flung high into the air. The sky overhead glowed and the wind whipped the smoke into strange shapes. Joe was transfixed. Never in his life had he seen such a huge fire. The biggest, a house fire he'd seen on the television, was nothing compared to this.

It was coming closer, but it wasn't moving all that fast. So the people who lived in the houses were able to escape. Still, there was something pitiless about the way it lapped from rooftop to rooftop, as unstoppable as the tide coming in.

"My bed!" screamed a woman. "Why didn't we move everything into the church, like I said? You said we should bring it here! You said the fire would be put out before it got this far! You said it would never reach your aunt's house!" The woman jabbed her finger at her husband with every accusation. "What was the point in moving it at all?" she shrieked. "Any minute now, everything will be lost!"

There was a flapping sound as curtains billowed out of the next door window. Tongues of flame licked all round them. The woman fell silent, and then began to cry.

With a shock, Joe realised how close the fire was now. It was getting dangerous! After all, this wasn't bonfire night, with ropes to keep you safe and wardens on watch. This was more like a bush fire. It was time to go.

He turned hurriedly, and began to make his way back along the street in the same direction as the rest of the crowd. Even though he was going with the flow, it was difficult to move quickly. Heap after heap of belongings lay on the ground, and the road was blocked by carts every few houses.

Joe squeezed past a frail old man being carried

out in his bed, and turned left up another street, hoping he was going the right way.

It wasn't until he reached Threadneedle Street that it dawned on him that he hadn't seen anyone trying to put the fire out. If that had been happening at home, there would have been fire engines with hoses, battering the flames with water. Here, he hadn't seen so much as a single bucket, even though there must have been taps in some of those houses.

As he came to Lucy's house, his footsteps faltered. What was he going to say to her family this time? Her parents must surely think him rude and ungrateful to have left without telling them, especially so soon after they'd welcomed him back.

He stood on the doorstep, trying to summon up courage. He had to trust that he would know what to say. It had always worked before.

He hadn't even touched the knocker, however, when the door opened.

"You've come!" Lucy exclaimed. "I hoped you would!" She seized his hands. "I'm afraid I got the time wrong," she whispered. "When you told me about the fire, there was so much else happening! I must have misremembered it. I was going to go. I was going to try and stop it! But it was too late."

Joe squeezed her hands. "Never mind. You're safe! That's the main thing. I've been so worried about you because of Tobias."

Before Lucy could answer, Joe heard Ellen's

voice. "Is someone there, Lucy? Who is it?"

His heart sank. Of course she wasn't alone in the house! Why else would she have been whispering?

"It's Joseph Hopkins, madam," Lucy called back to her mother. "Word must have reached him that Tobias has gone."

"What?! When?" Joe was incredulous. "What did you tell her this time?"

"I said I'd heard Tobias drag you out of the house," she muttered. "You *did* say to blame him, after all!" Her eyes twinkled. "I'll explain later."

She led the way through to the sitting room.

Joe had expected to find Ellen working at her embroidery frame, but she was packing the contents of the sideboard into a large wooden crate.

"Here you are again, Master Hopkins," she said with a tired smile. "You are very welcome, though we're not such merry company as when you were last here. London faces another great trial, as I'm sure you've seen. Where the plague destroyed its people, it looks as though this fire may swallow the city itself!"

She sank down into a chair and rubbed her face with her hands. "It's been burning for the best part of two days already, and grows more ferocious by the hour.

"But tell me, where have you been these last three weeks? What happened to you?"

12

Joe flicked a glance sideways at Lucy. It would have been good to talk to her before he had to answer. But it was too bad. He would just have to be vague and hope he didn't accidentally contradict what she'd told them.

"It seemed that Tobias didn't want me here, madam," he said cautiously.

"Lucy said he bundled you out of the house in the night," Ellen said. "I can't believe we didn't hear it! I don't know why she didn't wake us. We could have stopped him!"

"It wasn't quite like that," Joe said. "He asked me to go with him. I didn't like to say no. I told her not to wake you. I didn't want to disturb you. I didn't think it was anything serious." He shot another look at Lucy. She nodded.

"Well, she did wake us after you'd gone," Ellen said. "She was worried, and rightly so. We caught Tobias letting himself back into the house alone. He claimed he'd had no idea you were here! He denied having taken you anywhere. And then he came out with some fantastical story about you having vanished in front of him! But he refused to say what he wanted with you. In fact, he barely spoke another word from that night until he disappeared."

"When was that?" Joe asked.

"Yesterday morning. One of my husband's colleagues woke us early to tell us about the fire. The warehouses along the river had caught light already. It's been so windy. It was an inferno down there, with all the timber and hemp, and the tar and pitch for the ships. There were casks of oil, too, in one of the warehouses. That went up in minutes, my husband said. He went straight down to see if any of his stock could be saved. He took Tobias with him."

"But Tobias slipped away in the chaos," Lucy said, her voice heavy with meaning. "Nobody's seen him since."

Joe frowned. Tobias had talked about 'raining fire' on London. But his ambitions had been altogether grander. Was it possible that he'd abandoned his idea of a coordinated attack on king, parliament, and city, in favour of a simple baker's shop? That didn't sound like the Tobias he knew.

"At least you've come back," Ellen said, "though I must confess, I'm surprised to see you. Where have you been?"

"I wandered into the countryside," Joe said,

"through some of the villages." He thought quickly. "There was a kind old lady who gave me a bed and food in exchange for chopping wood and fetching water." That seemed plausible enough. He watched Lucy's mother carefully. She seemed to accept what he was saying.

Encouraged, he went on, "News of the fire reached me last night. I thought I must see if I could help you and your family. I felt bad that I'd left your house like that. I should have stood up to Tobias. I decided I'd come back, even though I thought it would mean facing him again."

Ellen paused, her hand half way to the packing box. "That is uncommonly kind!"

Joe realised she was on the edge of tears. Yet again, he hated himself for deceiving her.

He forced a smile. "It's the least I can do, after the kindness you've showed me."

Lucy's mother pulled herself together. "Would you mind, then, going out quickly to find out where the fire has got to, so that we know how much time we have? I hope we're safe for a while at least. But my husband went out at dawn and called by just before dinner to say there are many who've left it too late. We must be prepared, he said. He's gone with Peter to the Exchange. The stock in the warehouse was all lost, but at least what's in the shop can be saved."

"May I take Lucy with me?" Joe asked. "I don't know the names of the streets, so I wouldn't be able to describe to you where the fire is."

"Very well. But don't be too long. We need to pack up. And take care! I can't lose my only remaining daughter, and you do seem to have a habit of disappearing!" She smiled wanly.

This time, Lucy didn't waste a moment getting ready to leave the house. Outside the front door, she squeezed Joe's arm. "I'm so glad you came," she said. "I've been really wanting to go out and see what's happening, even though I know it might be dangerous. But my mother would never let me go alone!"

Joe grinned. "I'm happy to be here too," he said. He looked into Lucy's eyes. Something shifted in his chest. He dropped his gaze. "I just hope I manage to stay a bit longer this time," he said.

In the street, the crowd was denser than ever. Almost nobody was moving, despite a good deal of jostling and shouting. Joe sniffed the air. He didn't think the smell of smoke was any stronger here than it had been last time, but something had obviously happened to block the roads.

"Goodness!" Lucy exclaimed. "There's a pair of spinets on that cart, and another over there!"

"What are they?"

"Musical instruments. You know that painted box we have in the front room."

Joe remembered the thing Lucy had been playing like a piano the first time he'd come to the house. "I can only see one on the cart," he said, puzzled.

"It *is* only one," Lucy said.

"Oh, you mean like a pair of trousers?"

"What are trousers?"

Joe shook his head. "Forget it. It doesn't matter. Look there's someone in a bed. I saw another old man in his bed earlier."

"Poor things!" Lucy cried. "Imagine losing your home when you're so old and sick, you can't even get up and leave!"

"I don't understand why nobody's moving," Joe said. "It wasn't as bad as this before."

"Maybe there's a problem at the gate."

"What gate?"

"Bishopsgate – it's one of the gates in the city wall. There are eight. Bishopsgate isn't far up there." She gestured along the street to the right. At that moment, a small gap opened up in the crowd. At once, Lucy took her chance, and squeezed past a cart and along the street to the right, in the opposite direction from the way the crowds were going.

"So, where did you pop up when you reappeared?" she asked over her shoulder.

"Round behind the Pewterers' Hall," Joe answered. He kept as close behind her as he could. "I was more or less where we were when you left me, although Tobias did drag me out of the alley. I tried telling him I was his guardian angel, sent to stop him setting fire to London. I thought it was the only way to get him to give up the idea, if he thought God didn't want him to do it. But he didn't believe me. He said I'd have to help him start the fires. He was just pushing me back along the alley when I disappeared."

They stopped again, stuck behind a young man who was trying to manoeuvre an empty handcart the wrong way through the throng of people.

"So what Tobias told my parents about you vanishing was actually true?" Lucy asked.

"I guess so," Joe said. "He didn't recognise me in the alley. But I suppose once your parents started asking about me, he must have worked out that's who I was. Anyway, at least you got away. I've been so worried. Did he realise you'd been there with me?"

"I don't think so," Lucy said. "I did find those papers he was telling the others about. They were under a loose floorboard in his room."

"Where are they now?" Joe asked.

"Buried in the sand barrel in the kitchen."

"Why there? That's hardly the most obvious place to put them!"

"Exactly! Anyway, I didn't want to put them in my chamber, in case Tobias came looking for them – I didn't want him to know it was me who took them. And I couldn't put them in any of the other bedchambers because everyone was sleeping. I thought about the house of office, but there's nowhere really to put it in there, and anyway, he could easily search it while he was pretending to use the close-stool.

"The kitchen seemed best. It's usually quite busy, and he has no real excuse to go in there, except to wash his hands. When we've decided what to do with the papers, I'll move them."

At last, the handcart pushed on. Joe and Lucy stepped in behind it, letting the young man drive a path for them through the hoards of people.

"Does he know the plans are gone?" Joe asked.

"I'm sure he does," Lucy said. "I lay there listening after he'd come back. He waited until he thought everyone was asleep again, and then there was all sorts of scuffling, and the sound of things being moved in his room. He was trying to be quiet about it, but it sounded like he was getting more and more frantic. He was white as a sheet at breakfast the next morning."

"But he didn't say anything?"

Lucy shook her head.

"That's good, I suppose. It means he doesn't know it was you. I wonder what he thinks happened."

Lucy considered. "Maybe he thinks it was you. If you disappeared in front of him, he might think you'd reappeared back at our house, taken them, and vanished again."

Joe nodded. It was certainly possible. In fact, that was an idea he'd once made use of himself to trick Tobias, back in Jorvik.

"Or he might just think I'd found them already,"

he suggested, "and that was why I'd followed him to the meeting place."

They were still making very slow progress along the street. Perhaps this was a bad plan, Joe thought. The flames he'd seen earlier had been moving faster than this. At this rate, they might be overtaken by the fire before they had a chance to report back how far it had got.

"Did you tell anyone what Tobias was planning?" he asked.

"No." Lucy bit her lip. "I wanted to talk to you about it first. You do realise he could be hanged for plotting something like that, even though he didn't get as far as doing it?"

Joe swallowed. He didn't like Tobias at all. In fact, he loathed him. But he couldn't bring himself to wish the boy dead for something he hadn't actually done.

On the other hand, Tobias was a terrorist. You couldn't sit by and wait for terrorists to attack. Once you identified them, you had to do something.

"You don't think he started this fire, do you?" he asked.

Lucy was thoughtful. "I don't think he could have done, even if he wanted to. My father was so angry with him for going out in the night, and for forcing you to go with him, that he moved Solomon's perch to outside Tobias' bedroom door. Tobias couldn't have got out without Solomon screeching, unless he climbed out of the window. And if he did that, I'm not sure he'd have got back in, certainly not without Solomon hearing."

Joe suddenly realised there hadn't been the usual welcome from the monkey today. "Where is Solomon?"

"Gone," Lucy said. They had stopped again, pressed up against a house while another cart edged through. "It seems as though he sensed the fire somehow. Maybe he heard it or smelled it. Anyway, he waited until Peter let him off the leash yesterday, and then made straight for the kitchen window."

"Isn't that just coincidence?"

Lucy shook her head. "I don't think so. He could have done it any number of times – the windows have been open all summer because it's been so hot." She shrugged. "My father says it's an ill wind that blows no good."

Joe looked at her. "I don't understand."

"The fire may be coming, and my father has lost a lot already," Lucy said. "But on the positive side, he's not sorry to see the back of either Tobias or Solomon!" She grinned. "Peter was upset, though, about Solomon. He didn't find him as annoying as the rest of us!"

Finally, whatever had been holding up the crowd gave way, and people began to move forward more quickly. Lucy and Joe were able to move too, even though they were going against the tide.

Joe couldn't help feeling excited, even though he knew he should feel sorry for the people who'd already lost their homes, and those who were going to but didn't yet know it. Maybe Lucy's house would burn too. It seemed likely. And yet, he couldn't believe it. Bad things like that happened to other people, not to his friends or family.

Regardless of all of it, being in a crowd like this with her, and knowing they were both safe, he was exhilarated to be part of something big and important.

It still took them quite a while longer to reach the junction down at the Stocks Market. The street was less jammed here, because it was broader. But it felt more chaotic. People were hurrying in every direction rather than heading mostly the same way. There were a lot of shops being emptied here as well as houses, and still the endless heaps of possessions piled up in the street.

"It's no good," said a man nearby to his neighbour. "There just isn't a cart to be had! People are saying that carters from all around have driven into London to pick up the extra business. But I still can't find an empty one anywhere."

"It's the Dutch," said the other man grimly. "I heard they've bought most of them off. This is revenge for Terschellen. They want us to burn in our beds! So they're blocking the city gates to make sure we can't get out, and stopping the carters from coming in."

"It's not just the Dutch," a third man joined in.

"It's the French as well! They're in league with the Dutch against us!" He spat on the ground. "Filthy frogs! Didn't you hear, the bakers where it started is run by a Frenchman? He set fire to the place on purpose."

"That's not true," Joe muttered to Lucy. "It was an accident."

"Whatever it was," she replied, "we need to get on. My mother will be starting to worry soon."

But the three men had been joined by others. In seconds, quite a crowd of people had gathered, and Joe and Lucy were stuck right in the middle of them. The voices around them grew louder, each shouting to be heard over everyone else.

"I heard the baker had been planning it for a month!" cried someone.

"It's not the man who used to run the place," called someone else. "A Dutchman bought it for a small fortune just two weeks ago."

"I heard they haven't done any baking there for weeks."

"That's because it's a safe house for Catholic spies from France!"

"Didn't you hear, a ship came in on Saturday with only half its cargo? The rest was packed with Frenchmen. Hundreds of them in the hold!"

"I heard it was Dutchmen."

Joe and Lucy shrank down, unable to escape.

Then there was a cry. "There's one of the

scoundrels now!"

Abruptly, the crowd dissolved. Joe let his breath whistle through his teeth, relieved that he and Lucy could press on.

But then Lucy cried out. "Oh no!"

Joe followed her gaze. The mob had surged along the street and surrounded a man on his own who was dressed slightly differently to everyone else. There was shouting, and almost at once, fists began to fly.

In the middle of the mob, the foreigner put his arms up over his head. A few seconds later, he slipped from view. But still the mob raged around him, punching and kicking wildly.

At last, their fury spent, the men stepped back. Joe saw one brush the dirt from his hands. Several straightened their clothes, and another turned away, red-faced. Two crowed triumphantly.

In less than a minute, they had dispersed to their houses and shops.

Beneath his crumpled cloak, their victim lay still. As Joe and Lucy watched, blood seeped out from underneath his hat, making a puddle on the dry ground.

13

"Poor man!" Lucy said. Her face was pale.

Joe started to move towards the heap on the ground. His friend grabbed his sleeve. She shook her head.

"But we can't just leave him!" Joe cried.

"We have to!"

"At least we should check if he's alright! And what about the police? Somebody should report it."

"What's a police?"

"Oh, for goodness' sake!" Worry made Joe snap. "The people who enforce the law!"

Lucy glared at him. "The constable of the parish will be much too busy with the fire!" she said irritably.

"An ambulance then, or a doctor!"

Again, Lucy shook her head. "We've no money to pay for a doctor, and he mightn't be able to pay himself. We have to leave him, really Joe. His wife will clean him up."

"But what if he can't get himself home to her?"

Joe protested. "You saw how they were kicking him! What if they've ruptured something inside him? He could bleed to death! He might even get run over before he can get up!" He pulled away from Lucy again.

"Joe! Don't!" Her voice was sharp. There was fear in her face. "You don't want those men to think we're Dutch sympathisers, do you?"

Joe looked round. The two men who'd been crowing were watching them coldly. He hesitated. Grown men didn't usually beat up children, did they? Yet, Lucy obviously thought they might.

He hesitated. He felt like a coward, giving up so easily. But perhaps she was right. Perhaps he really would be asking for trouble.

Reluctantly, he let her steer him away. When he looked over his shoulder again, the beaten man had got onto his hands and knees and was crawling back the way he'd come.

It was vile, Joe thought, the way people looked for a scapegoat when they were scared or angry, the way they ganged up together. Not one of those men would have dared to do it alone! He felt sick, frightened, and furious all at once.

Suddenly, from not far away, there was a tremendous crash.

"God save us!" Lucy cried. "What was that?"

They spun round in time to see the burning spire of a church topple over. There was a roar like an avalanche.

"The churches! The churches!" shrieked a woman. "We're all doomed!" She began to grab her possessions from the ground. Around them, everyone was running to and fro. A horse bolted, breaking free from the cart it was hitched to. The driver yelled. Boxes tumbled. People leapt out of the way.

"Flames!" Lucy cried. "There they are! Just over there!"

Joe felt a stab of panic. They'd come a lot closer to the fire than he'd realised. He'd got so used to the background crackling and the acrid smoke, that he'd stopped paying attention.

"Look! They're pulling that house down!" He pointed.

Along the street to their left, men with long poles and ropes were dragging the frame of a house to the ground.

"Why are they doing that?" Lucy wailed.

"Where are the fire engines?" Joe cried. "Why aren't they pumping water? You have taps, don't you?"

Lucy didn't answer.

"Come on!" It was Joe's turn to pull her away. "We have to get back. I'm not sure your mother has as much time as she thought."

They pushed and scrambled through the crowd once more, back up Threadneedle Street. Beyond the buildings on their right, they could hear the fire clearly now. Fear swelled inside Joe. He'd been so excited to be part of history. How had he not realised it would be like this?

As they burst into the house, Ellen was in the hallway. "Thank God, you're back!" she exclaimed. "I was so worried! I was going to come and look for you. It's madness out there! I shouldn't have asked you to go!"

Lucy leaned on the front door, her eyes closed.

"Are you alright?" Her mother stooped to look into her face. "Lucy? What's happened?" She looked round at Joe. "What did you see?"

"It's quite frightening," Joe said, trying to sound calmer than he felt. "We watched a foreigner get beaten up, and there were men pulling a house down. People are running around like crazy, and a church fell down not far from where we were."

"Which one?"

"St. Stephen Walbrook," Lucy answered. Her voice was high and strange. "The fire's nearly at Poultry." She shook her head. "It's all being swallowed up, our whole world, everything I know, everywhere we've always gone!" She started to cry.

Joe stood awkwardly as Ellen put her arms around Lucy. He longed to hug her too. But he knew that would seem odd.

At last, she dried her eyes. "I know there's no use crying," she sniffed.

"It's only buildings," Ellen said gently. "Only things. None of that matters as much as people. We've lived through the worst already."

"But these things," Lucy gulped, "this house, it's all we have left since the others died."

"And each other," Ellen reminded her. "We still have each other. Anyway, we haven't lost our home yet. We may be lucky. But just in case, let's carry on packing up. Then, even if we lose the roof over our heads, we won't lose everything."

At that moment, there was a loud knock on the door behind Lucy. They all jumped.

"Mr. Waters!" Ellen said, as she opened the door. "What can we do for you?"

"We've come to help you, Mistress Lucas," the man said. "The Master says we're to take the larger pieces of furniture and anything else that's ready."

"That's very kind of you," Lucy's mother replied. "I'm sure you have better things to do than help us."

"Not at all, Mistress. It's an honour. The Master specially wanted men he could trust. They say there are carters who've vanished with entire loads."

Ellen was aghast. "Imagine that! It would be unbearable, after all this!"

She turned to one room and then the other, beset by indecision. "I suppose the beds should go first," she said. "They're the most valuable. Then perhaps the tables and chairs, and if there's room, the spinets and the sideboards."

At once, Mr. Waters summoned his men from the street. A while later, after a good deal of banging, they carried the first section of a four-poster bed down the narrow stairs.

"Lucy, Joe," Ellen said, "could you please pack up the bed covers and unfasten the tapestries from their tenterhooks. When that's done, you could take down the curtains. I had to let Mary and Elizabeth go home, so we need to manage on our own."

"Will we not stay here tonight?" Lucy asked.

"I don't know. Last evening, the fire had only just reached Cannon Street. Yet from what you've told me, it must be all the way up Walbrook now. We'll decide when your father returns. I don't know where he's planning to take everything anyway, or where we'll go if the worst happens."

A chill ran through Joe at her words.

"There's no good worrying," Ellen said briskly. "We can only do our best, and trust in God for the rest."

What remained of the afternoon passed in a whirl of activity. Lucy's mother directed the men carrying the family's possessions out to the waiting carts, while Joe and Lucy packed the things she'd asked into two large chests. Then they rolled up the rugs, took down the pictures and mirrors, and collected together the books, a globe, and the few other ornaments the family owned.

After that, they all worked together packing up the kitchen. Nobody spoke much. Joe felt deep contentment to be with Lucy again. But it didn't seem right to make small talk, knowing that just a few streets away, the flames were eating their way towards them. Back at home, he'd tried to work out whether Lucy's house would be spared. But on the clearest map he'd found, the fire had burned a good deal of Threadneedle Street. Without knowing exactly how far along the road this house was, he couldn't tell whether it would survive.

The evening was subdued. The carts had gone, and Lucy's father came back with Peter for just long enough to eat a supper of bread, cheese and cold beef. Then he left again, having scarcely remarked on Joe's presence except to say, with a quizzical look, that he hoped Joe would be able to stay longer this time.

Peter stayed behind now, but he was too exhausted to talk much. Ellen fretted around the house, wrapping odds and ends in scraps of cloth and tucking them into boxes.

At bedtime, they all lay down to sleep on two palliasses on the floor of the now empty dining room. It was like being back at Fishbourne, Joe thought, feeling the sharp ends of straw poking through the bag it had been stuffed into. At least his clothes stopped the worst of the scratchiness, though. By unspoken agreement, they had all decided to sleep fully dressed, ready to leave if they had to.

For what felt like a long time, Joe lay awake, listening to Peter snoring. It was stifling hot, even with the windows open, and there was a lot of shouting and rumbling of wheels from the street. The low roar of the fire was constant now, and the sky between the buildings was bright yellow, with no sign of darkness falling. He couldn't see how he would ever fall asleep.

But the next thing he knew, Lucy was shaking him awake.

"We have to go," she said. "My father says the fire's broken through onto Cheapside. The Royal Exchange is burning. They say even St. Paul's will go up!"

Blearily, Joe fumbled his way into his coat and shoes. He had no idea what time it was. The sky was even brighter than before, though more orange now than yellow.

In the hallway, William Lucas was overseeing the men carrying the remaining furniture and boxes out to another cart. His face was grey with fatigue.

Joe found Ellen and Lucy in the kitchen, spreading bread with butter for them to take.

"Where are we going?" Lucy asked her mother.

"Your father knows someone with a country house out at Bethnal Green," Ellen said. "That's where the furniture went yesterday."

Joe was about to say that Bethnal Green wasn't in the country, but stopped himself. It obviously was in this world.

"Have some whey, Joe," Lucy said, handing him a cup. The liquid was yellowish and tasted bitter. But he drank it back.

William strode in. "I'm going to leave you to make your way with the cart," he said. "They need more men over at the Tower. The wind has changed. It's blowing eastward now. They're afraid the fire will reach the gunpowder stores."

Ellen clung to him. "Must you really go?"

"The King and the Duke of York have been manning the pumps," William said. "If they're not too great to help, I'm certainly not. I'm only glad I moved everything from the shop yesterday. There were plenty who thought I was being hasty, or who moved their stock to one of the churches. They've lost everything now."

"Do please take care!" Ellen begged him.

"God will protect me, if that's His plan," William answered. He kissed his wife's hair and squeezed Lucy's shoulder.

"Peter," he said, "you are the man of the house. I entrust to you the task of bringing your mother, your sister and our guest to safety." He shook Peter's hand, nodded once more to them all, and left.

Joe looked at Lucy, and then at Ellen. Lucy was white. Her mother was blinking back tears. The kitchen was empty now except for a couple of barrels beside the back door.

"Very well," Ellen said unsteadily. "There's no point delaying." She shepherded them all out of the house to the waiting cart.

Outside, the street was now completely blocked.

Joe wondered how the cart had managed to get through at all. The air was thick with smoke. His eyes prickled. His tongue shrank in his mouth. The roar of the flames was loud now behind the shouting and crying of all the people desperate to escape.

He climbed up onto the cart behind Lucy, and perched on a box. Two men and a boy sat at the front with the carter.

"Ready to go, madam?"

The cart began to creep forward. But it was incredibly slow, no more than a few centimetres at a time. The horse's ears flicked back and forth, and it shifted its hooves, impatient to take proper steps. After a quarter of an hour, they were still only two houses further along.

"This is awful!" Ellen cried. "Whatever is going on?"

"It's the gates, Mistress," said Mr. Waters. "There are so many people trying to get out of the city, and some still trying to get in, just as we were earlier, coming to fetch this load."

"At this rate, the fire will catch up with us all!"

"If you'd prefer to walk, Mistress, we'll stay with the cart and make sure everything gets to where it's going."

"I think we will," Ellen said. "I can't bear to sit up here not moving."

At once, Peter jumped down and offered his hand to his mother. Lucy followed, and Joe climbed down beside her.

"We should try to stay together," Ellen said. "But if we do get separated, there's a hostelry straight up the road from Bishopsgate. It's called The Royal Oak. It's less than half a mile from the city walls. We'll meet there."

With Peter at the front, they began to make their way through the crowd. It was slow going, scarcely any quicker than the cart. It was difficult, too, not to trip on broken cobbles, since they couldn't see where they were treading.

Suddenly, Lucy gave a shout. "The barrel! I forgot! Did we bring the sand from the kitchen?"

"Sand?" Ellen called back. "No, there was no room on the cart. Don't worry. We can afford to lose that!"

"No! I have to go back!"

Before anyone could stop her, Lucy spun round and squeezed past Joe.

"Lucy! Stop!" Ellen cried. "It doesn't matter!"

But it was too late.

"I'll go with her," Joe called. With a clutch of his heart, he knew what Lucy had remembered. How could they have forgotten? Without Tobias' plans, they'd never be able to prove what he'd been plotting. There might be no point now, but they still should have brought them, just in case.

"We'll catch up with you in a few minutes," he called to Ellen, hoping it was true. Then he turned to force his way back through the people behind him.

It was near to impossible! Joe found himself jammed up against stomachs and beneath chins, wedged into doorways and crushed against wheels. The crowd was never-ending.

Sometimes, people moved apart to go around him, as though he was a rock in the middle of a river. But mostly, he was just swept backwards, away from Lucy's house.

Yet somehow, Lucy herself seemed to be making progress. People must be letting her through. He saw the back of her head appear now and then, getting further and further away. Then he couldn't see her any more.

Later on, back in his own world, he tried to think whether there was any way he could have known what was going to happen next. The roaring of the fire was the same, no louder than it had been when they'd stepped out of the house. Nothing obvious changed. But panic began to spread through the crowd.

Joe saw it on the faces of the people coming towards him. They pushed past him roughly now. Shouts went up, complaints from those further ahead that there was nowhere to go and no point shoving. Swiftly, the pitch of the shouting grew shriller.

Joe called Lucy's name, but couldn't make out an answer. Again, he yelled, at the top of his voice this time. A woman who'd been pressed up face to face with him yelled right back, angry and afraid. Joe flinched. Lucy didn't reply.

Joe's arms were pinned to his sides now. He was further away than he'd started out. It was hopeless! He would have to give up! There was no sense in trying to go against the flow, no chance at all of getting to Lucy now. He would have to hope she made it to the house and back out again safely.

He turned back in the direction the crowd was moving. There was a sudden shove from behind. Joe staggered forward. His chin was thrust into the back of the man in front of him. Even the tiniest spaces between people and carts had closed up now. The crowd began to surge forward.

Behind Joe, there was a scream. He wanted to turn round, but couldn't move his shoulders. He craned his neck. Someone had fallen. He didn't think it was Lucy. She'd been further back than that. The crowd surged again. A horse reared up, its hooves flailing the air. Someone else fell. There were two voices screaming, then three, then four.

Joe's ears rang. Everywhere, there was shouting and crying. He heard more screams as people stumbled. Wheels shifted on cobbles. Limbs and bodies were crushed. And always the terrible pressure from behind, squeezing, squeezing.

He fought for breath. He had to keep on his feet. If he tripped, he would be trampled. He made himself concentrate on breathing, on staying afloat in the sea of people carrying him forward. His shoes sank into something soft beneath them.

There was another shove and a cracking sound. He gasped and tried to brace his arms against the person in front of him. It was like drowning. The pressure on his chest. The desperate need for air. Then a sudden, awful silence.

Dimly, he realised that something had changed. There was space. He was moving freely. Yet he still couldn't breathe. Then he felt himself lifted up. He erupted into noise and light and confusion. And air! Sweet life-giving air!

Someone or something propelled him along. He rubbed his eyes. Three green figures hovered in front of him. One was holding something red and white.

Joe allowed himself to be hauled out of the swimming pool and laid down on the cold tiles. Another person in green climbed out of the pool. They were lifeguards, he realised, these green people.

They put a towel over him and began asking him questions. He heard his mother's name over the tannoy. He groaned.

"It happened again, didn't it?" Mum said, a few minutes later, as she knelt beside him on the poolside.

"No," Joe lied. "I dived too deep and hit my head." Realising this sounded unlikely, he added, "I think someone kicked me by accident."

Mum looked up at the lifeguards.

"We didn't notice anything unusual," said the

one who'd rescued Joe. "He just went still in the water, then seemed to be having trouble getting back to the surface."

"I'm fine, honestly, Mum," Joe insisted. He avoided her eye as she helped him up.

"I'm right outside," she said, at the changing room door. "Shout if you have a problem. Though, of course, you don't shout when this happens. I know that now." She sounded both cross and unhappy.

Joe sat down on the bench in the cubicle and put his head in his hands. Somehow, he had to find a way of managing this better. He had to try not to get back into Lucy's world except when he was alone.

Like a shaft of light, he saw in his mind the street he'd been in just a few minutes ago: the crowd pressing forward, the terrified horse, people crammed against each other, against buildings and carts. Screaming mouths, gaps opening as people fell, then closing over. The crowd pressing forward again, the hideous softness of bodies under foot.

He covered his face with his hands. The books had all said that hardly anyone had died in the Great Fire of London. But what if they were wrong?

The terror and stress Joe had been holding back exploded inside him. He burst into tears.

14

It was the worst summer holiday Joe had ever had, including last year, when Dad had just moved out.

There were more pointless tests at the hospital, and a referral for September to some observation centre where Joe was going to be monitored for a week.

"You're so lucky, getting time off school!" Sam said enviously.

But the idea of being shut up in a room with wires stuck to his head day and night didn't sound like much fun to Joe. School was better than that, even on a bad day.

He and Sam went to stay with Dad for a week in the middle of August. Dad had a much nicer place now than the horrible little flat he'd moved into last summer. But Joe was too miserable to enjoy any of the things they did together.

The more time that went by, the more convinced he was that Lucy had died trying to escape the fire.

The crush had been bad enough for him to be pulled home into his own time. But she'd been further back in the crowd, nearer to the source of the panic. He imagined her being squashed like he'd been, the air forced out of her lungs. He pictured her slight body pressed flat, slipping down beneath the tide of feet.

If only she would call him back into her world! He ached to know that she was alright. Over and over, he relived those last terrible moments – the screams of the people who stumbled, the hole in the noise when each scream stopped, crushed into silence by feet, hooves, wheels.

At last, he couldn't bear it any more. He decided to try speaking to Dad.

He waited till Sam was busy with his games console in another room before bringing up the subject. It wasn't going to be easy to talk about without getting upset.

"Do you know much about the Great Fire of London?" he began.

His father looked up from his laptop and grinned. "I was wondering when you were going to give me a history update! The Great Fire now, is it? That's not such a leap as before. It was Tudors at Easter, wasn't it? So you've just hopped over the Gunpowder Plot and the Civil War, and the Plague, of course. Quite big hops, perhaps ..."

"I know, I know." Joe was impatient. "The thing is, I've been reading some books about the fire, and they all say that only six people were killed, even though four fifths of London burnt down. I was just wondering, is that really right, do you think?"

Dad sat up in his chair. Joe could see he was really listening now. "That's a very good question," he said. "You'll make a good historian one day, if you choose, challenging received wisdom like that."

Joe looked at his feet. "It just doesn't seem very likely, that's all."

"You're right," Dad agreed. "It doesn't. For one thing, there was another big fire in London four hundred years earlier which killed three thousand people, even though the city wasn't nearly as densely built. So no, I'm not sure we can be all that certain. After all, no Bill of Mortality was published that week."

"No bill what?"

"Bill of Mortality. They were lists of how many people had died in each district in the last seven days. There's one that crops up over and over, from one of the worst plague weeks. Let's have a look."

Joe stood behind him while he searched on Google.

"Here it is. September 1665." Dad pointed. "See here, over seven thousand people died that week from the plague. But look, two died of a cough, three were 'frighted', three died of grief, and one just died 'suddenly', it says."

"But that's daft!" Joe exclaimed. "How would

you die of any of those things?"

"You wouldn't. We know that now. But they didn't have our medical knowledge, remember. So the 'frighted' ones might have died of heart attacks, as might the 'suddenly' person. The coughs could have been a symptom of tuberculosis, and the grief was probably something else altogether. It could have been cancer, for example, and it just happened that the person died soon after they'd been bereaved."

Joe nodded.

"There's another thing about these lists, though," Dad went on. "The information was collected by 'searchers', who were mostly poor, elderly women, who went from house to house. The family of the dead person had to pay the searcher to record the information. You can imagine that if they didn't want her to write down that it was plague, they might pay her a bit extra to put something else."

Joe thought of Lucy's family, shut up in their house for three months. He could see why people would do that.

"Why wasn't there a list for the week of the fire?" he asked.

Before Dad could reply, he knew the answer.

"Think of the chaos of everyone trying to escape," Dad said. "And think about who the searchers were – the old and poor would have been the least likely to get away. Even if they did, they'd be too busy trying to save what little they had. And then the encampments outside the city, where a lot of people landed up, were probably a bit like refugee camps today, everyone all muddled up together. It would have been impossible!"

"Wouldn't people say, though," Joe asked, "if they'd left someone behind, or one of their family had been killed in the crush?"

"Not if nobody came to ask," Dad said. "There was no registry office to go to and report deaths."

Joe's heart sank. "What about bodies?" he asked. "If a lot of people did die, wouldn't their remains have been found?"

"In a fire like that?" Dad raised an eyebrow. "Samuel Pepys mentions the ruins still smoking five months later. In that heat, the bodies would have got cremated." He sat back. "There was another diarist, John Evelyn, who wrote about how dirty and dangerous London normally was, how people got killed falling under carts in the narrow streets. Just think what it must have been like in the crush of people fleeing the flames! It would have been so easy to get trampled." He looked up at Joe. "What's the matter? You've gone white!" He jumped up from his chair and put his arms around Joe. "Have I upset you? I'm really sorry! What a sensitive soul you are!"

Joe buried his face in Dad's shirt and held his breath, determined not to cry. It wasn't Dad's fault that he'd casually confirmed Joe's worst fears.

"Why didn't they try to put the fire out?" Joe

asked, when he'd got control of himself.

"They did. But it had been a long, hot summer, it was very windy, and the buildings were very close together. They couldn't get much water on the fire, either, like we can today."

"But I didn't see -" Joe stopped.

"- anything in the books about it?" finished Dad helpfully. "Well, they had water pipes down the roads, but once they'd been broken open to fill a few buckets, the water pressure disappeared. They tried sand and dirt, and milk, even wee, I read somewhere. But it was no match for a fire like that."

"What about the King manning the pumps?" Joe asked, remembering William's remark.

"He did," Dad said. "But the pumps only held about four pints, even though they took two or three men to work them. Imagine three men squirting the equivalent of one medium-sized bottle of milk at a house fire! It's laughable, isn't it?"

"And there weren't fire engines?"

"Not like today. There were a few, but they were huge, so it would have been more or less impossible to get them through the streets, even without everyone fleeing. And although they had pumps, they had no hoses. They had to fill up from the river. One even fell in trying to get water! No, the one thing that might have made the difference was if they'd started pulling down houses to make firebreaks."

"But they did, didn't they?" Joe said cautiously.

"Not quickly enough. A lot of the people who lived in the houses were tenants, just like now. The Mayor of London didn't dare pull houses down as a safety measure, in case he upset the rich owners who'd gone off to the country.

"By the time the King overruled him, the streets were too crowded and they couldn't clear the timber away. So the fire just crossed the gaps and carried on burning."

Joe sank down on the sofa. It sounded as though Lucy and her family hadn't stood a chance after all. If only he'd persuaded them to leave London before the fire began. Why hadn't he thought of that?

"There's one other interesting thing about the fire," Dad said. "The baker, whose oven supposedly started it, claimed it wasn't his fault. Of course, you can see why he'd say that. He was being blamed for one of the worst disasters in English history. But in fact, someone else did confess to it."

Joe sat up, alert at once. In the confusion, he'd forgotten all about Tobias. Perhaps Tobias *had* done it. Perhaps he'd got caught and confessed.

"Who was it?" The question sprang out.

Dad looked surprised. "A French watchmaker called Robert Hubert."

Joe's shoulders sagged.

"The curious thing isn't so much that his confession was false," Dad said. "Throughout history, people have been tortured into confessing to all sorts of things they haven't done. But he chose to confess without torture to something he couldn't possibly have done. It turned out later he was on a ship at the time, not even in London. And it was a hopeless confession! He didn't know where or when the fire had started, and he changed his story each time he found out a bit more. I mean, people do that, change their stories. But that's usually when they're claiming they *didn't* commit a crime, not trying to convince people they *did*."

"What happened to him?" Joe asked.

"He was hanged," Dad said. "It suited the government to have someone to blame. And the crowd was so wild for a scapegoat that when the body was cut down, they tore it apart before it could be handed over to the authorities to dispose of."

Joe nodded. It wasn't hard to imagine a mob venting their anger on the corpse of the person who'd confessed, after what he'd seen done to the innocent Dutchman. He pulled a face. "I'm glad I didn't live back then," he said, as a way of closing the conversation.

"Me too," Dad agreed.

For the rest of the summer holidays, Joe felt listless and sad. He tried to come to terms with the idea that Lucy was gone, dead, that he would never travel back in time again. But he simply couldn't get over it, especially since he couldn't talk to anyone about it.

"I think he might be suffering from depression," Joe heard his mum say to her friend, on the phone. "It's strange. I thought he'd coped okay with me and Steve splitting up last year. But he seems worse now than he was at the start. You know he started having these seizures last autumn. Well, they're getting more frequent."

Joe crept away. He didn't want to hear any more.

That evening, Mum came and sat down on his bed just before he turned his light off. Unusually for her, she came straight to the point.

"Tell me what's wrong, Joe," she said.

Joe tried to think of something he could say that would answer the question adequately. But there wasn't anything. "Nothing's wrong," he said.

"You're not yourself though, are you?" she said gently. "You've been so quiet. You don't seem to want to do anything, not even read your history books." She gave him a half-hearted smile.

"There's no point," Joe said. The words came out more bitterly than he'd meant them to.

Mum looked taken aback. "That's not true! I know I tease you about it, but I'm proud of you for being so interested in it. It's much better than Sam's endless computer games, and you've learnt such a lot!"

Joe shrugged. There *was* no point. If Lucy was dead, he would never go back in time again. He'd lost his St. Christopher so there would never be another world, and in any case, he didn't want to go anywhere if she wasn't there.

At that moment, he was aware of a hissing in his ears. He swallowed to clear them, but it didn't go away.

His heart leapt. If this was Lucy calling him, she couldn't be dead after all! He beamed.

"That's better," Mum said. "It's good to see you smile again. You're a good boy, Joe!"

He lay back on his pillow, praying she would leave quickly. "Goodnight, Mum," he said, hoping his voice still sounded normal.

She reached over and switched off the light. "Night, Joe. Sleep well."

Her words came to him as though through a fog. He blinked.

He was on Threadneedle Street again. And it *was* recognisably Threadneedle Street.

Joe felt a rush of relief. The fire couldn't have reached where he was standing because there were still buildings on both sides of the road. Their fronts were now black with soot, and ash lay in heaps at the foot of them like drifts of dirty snow. But they still almost touched overhead, just as they had done before.

In the middle of the street, a path had been trodden down, the ash packed in between the cobbles, making the road pale and flat. The smell of burning was still pungent.

A woman came out of one of the houses

carrying a wooden bucket, and began cleaning her windows. Joe wondered what time it was and what day. Other than the woman, the street was deserted. The strip of sky overhead was grey – perhaps smoke had blotted out the sun, he thought – and yet it was somehow much lighter than he expected. He frowned and turned around to look for Lucy's house.

His breath caught in his throat.

His brain hadn't just been telling him that it was light, but that it was *too* light. A few houses along from where he was standing, the buildings stopped, raggedly, trailing off into mounds of charred timbers. Beyond, a wide expanse of sky stretched over a desolate landscape.

He moved down the street in a daze, fascinated by the devastation ahead of him. Charcoal spikes and crags of tumbled stone rose out of a sea of soft, grey ash. Strange, tall stalks poked up in twos and threes all over the place, like trees struck by lightning. They must have been chimneys, Joe realised. The bricks were black, but they hadn't burned like everything else.

Figures drifted around in the ruins, tiny against the vastness of this new wasteland. All over the place, smoke trickled up into the sky from smouldering wood. Joe narrowed his eyes to peer through the grey pall that hung in the air. He could see what must be the river, half a mile away. Beyond Lucy's street, there was not one building standing in what should have been a city crammed with life.

He looked carefully at the last remaining houses on Threadneedle Street. The golden pheasant sign was nowhere to be seen, and the glass in all the windows was clouded by smoke and ash, so he couldn't peer in. He had no idea whether one of these houses was Lucy's.

Where the street broke off, he picked his way onwards. He could feel heat coming off the ground, like from a pavement on a really hot summer's day. Here and there, embers glowed orange.

Joe kept his eyes on the ground ahead, wary of treading on nails or shards of glass in the ash. In one place, there was a kind of hard, dark grey puddle. He crouched down to look at it. It was smooth, but too hot to touch. Melted lead perhaps, he thought. One of the churches might have been here.

His progress was slow, not having a street to follow. After a while, he began to wonder why he was bothering.

There was no sign of Lucy, although he passed people here and there, like ghosts in the smoke. Some were trying to move bricks or what was left of wooden beams. One man was digging where his garden must have been. But mostly people just stared open-mouthed at the empty air where their houses had stood.

One figure Joe passed was crouching down, busy with something on the ground. He didn't seem to be digging or trying to move anything. Joe wondered idly what else he might be doing, but didn't stop to ask.

In the far distance, a shadow appeared through the smoke, climbing over the rubble, just like Joe was. The air was too hazy to see clearly, but it had to be a girl, because she was hampered by her skirts. As she came closer, and the shape of her became more solid, Joe saw that her head was bowed. There was an air of utter dejection about her.

The girl paused for a moment and looked up, apparently searching for anything she recognised. Joe's heart skipped a beat. Wasn't that Lucy? He'd guessed she must be alive, if it was her who'd called him back. But she should have been safe at Bethnal Green with her family.

This certainly looked like her though, wandering forlornly through the ruins. He quickened his pace, scrambling over mounds of stone and brick. As he hurried through the ash, pale flakes rose up in a cloud around his feet, still warm from the fire.

"Lucy!" he called. His voice sounded loud in the stillness. But the girl didn't look up.

Joe hurried on. He was almost sure it was her.

"Lucy?"

She raised her head.

"Joe? Is that you?" Her voice quavered. "Is that really you?"

15

In less than a minute, Joe had covered the remaining distance between them. As he reached Lucy, he hesitated for a split-second. Then he put his arms around her.

She hugged him so tightly he could hardly breathe. "Joe!" she wept into his shoulder. "You're alive! You survived! I thought you'd been killed!"

Joe's heart thundered.

"I thought the same about you," he managed to say. He felt choked.

He unwound his arms and stepped back. "It was awful, wasn't it?" He bit his lip. What a stupid thing to say! But what was the point in describing the horror? Lucy knew perfectly well what he meant.

She nodded numbly.

"Did Peter and your parents …?" He didn't know how to finish the question.

"I don't know." She clasped her hands together.

He was struck by how small and fragile she

looked.

"I haven't seen them since I last saw you. I've come back to see if there's anything left. I thought if there was – if our house had survived … But without any of the old streets and buildings –" She waved a hand helplessly. "I can't believe it! I've lived here all my life, and I'm completely lost!"

"What happened to you all meeting outside the city walls?"

Lucy blinked and swallowed. "There was such a crush, not just on this side but outside the gate, too. You know what it was like near our house, the people who fell -" She broke off.

Joe nodded.

She took a deep breath and went on, "Outside, it was hardly any better. Before I knew what had happened, I'd been swept up in the crowd. I don't really know how. But I ended up at Moorfields. There's a huge encampment up there." She wiped her eyes with her sleeve. The frilled cuff was filthy. Her cheeks and forehead were smudged with soot, Joe noticed, and her hair was knotted and grey from the ash, her white cap gone.

"I've been wandering over the fields for the last three days, hoping to find them," she said. "But there are hundreds, maybe even thousands of people sheltering up there. It's hopeless!"

"Did you try Bethnal Green?" Joe asked. "Wasn't that where your family was going?"

"I don't know where it is." She sniffed. "I've no idea how long it would take me to walk there. I suppose if the house has gone …" Again, her voice trailed off.

Joe put his hand tentatively on her arm. "I know where Threadneedle Street is," he said. "That's where I was when I reappeared. Some of the houses are still standing, though I don't know if yours is one of them. I'll take you there."

He turned around, back the way he'd come, and gulped. From this direction, there was a kind of ring of buildings around the ash, marking the edge of the fire's progress. He'd headed out across the wasteland without a backward look, and it wasn't obvious at all now which was Lucy's street.

He cleared his throat and set out towards the point he thought he'd come from. Hopefully, Lucy would recognise where she was when they got close, even if he didn't find the right street straight away.

She was quiet as they crossed the ruins together. Joe stole a look at her every now and then. He wanted to speak but didn't know what to say. She had seemed glad to see him, but now her expression had closed up again. He wished he could do something to take her sadness away. For his own part, he was overjoyed to find that she'd survived. But her happiness depended on finding her home still standing and her family alive.

Abruptly, she stopped. She grabbed his arm.

"What is it? What's the matter?"

She pointed to a figure crouching down a short way away. It was the boy Joe had seen fiddling with something on the ground. Now, he was looking at a stick he held in his hand. It was wound round with rope at one end. Flames danced over the surface of the rope.

"Tobias!" Joe gasped. "I passed him earlier, but I didn't recognise him! He looks so scruffy. And he's cut off his hair."

Lucy nodded.

"I couldn't think what he was doing," Joe whispered. "He must have been trying to light that torch. But whatever for?"

They looked at each other. Fear sparked in the pit of Joe's stomach. "The plans," he murmured. "He's going to see if your house is still there, and look for his plans. Did you manage to get them, when you went back?"

She shook her head. "The crowd was too tight. I never made it to the house. What shall we do?" Her voice rose. "If the house didn't burn down, he's bound to find them! The sand barrel is almost the only thing left."

"Could we go round a different way, try and get there first?" Joe suggested. But even as he said it, he knew it was nonsense. There was no different way across the open ground.

In any case, it was already too late. Tobias stood up and looked straight at them. The muscles of his face went rigid.

Then he screeched, "Demon!"

Joe felt Lucy shrink away. But Tobias wasn't looking at her. He stalked across the embers, his eyes locked on Joe's face.

"Demon!" he screamed again, brandishing the flaming torch. Behind the glow, he was pale with rage. "You said you were my guardian angel! But you're a servant of the devil!"

Joe steeled himself. He would not be terrorised by this boy, despite the fire he carried.

"If I'm a demon," he called back, "why am I here now?"

"To turn me from the path of righteousness again!" Tobias glowered. "You stopped me once. Now you want to stop me a second time!"

"You're surely not going to burn down Whitehall and Westminster, are you?" Joe asked, incredulous. "Not after this!" He made himself take his eyes off Tobias, as though he didn't need to watch him, and looked out over the smoking city.

When he looked back, Tobias was several steps closer. His mouth was twisted into a grim smile. "Maybe not," he said, "though it saddens me to see such a wicked and lustful king escape unharmed."

Joe watched him advancing. His mind raced, trying to come up with a plan.

"The thing is," Tobias snarled, "that same king will have me killed if my plans are discovered. I never should have written them down! But they were so complicated, the tides, the timings, exactly where and at what hour each element should be executed. Nothing had been left to chance!"

Joe detected a note of pride beneath Tobias' fury.

"It would have succeeded too, if it hadn't been for you!" Tobias' voice rose to a screech. "And then you vanished, and the plans vanished with you!"

He was only a few steps away now. Joe felt the heat of the torch on his face.

He stood his ground. His heart was pounding. "I wasn't the only person who knew there were plans," he said, as steadily as he could. "What about the boys who were supposed to help you, the ones who ran off?"

Tobias stopped. There was a fractional pause. Then he growled, "They wouldn't have dared! And they couldn't have found them – they'd never set foot in the house before! Whereas you -" He thrust the torch towards Joe. "You'd already ingratiated yourself with the master and mistress, already imposed your lies on them!"

"No!" Lucy shouted.

Joe turned in surprise.

"He didn't!" Her eyes were ablaze with indignation. "The lies were mine, not his. And my parents liked him because he's friendly and decent, and appreciative, which is more than you've ever been!"

The full glare of Tobias' loathing swung round

onto her. "Defending the devil, Mistress Lucy?" he snapped. "Lucifer keeps a special place in hell for sinners like you! Next, you'll say that your demon friend didn't steal my plans!"

Joe kept his gaze fixed on Tobias' face, determined not to look at Lucy.

But she must have given herself away, because the older boy suddenly screeched at her. "It was *you*! The demon sent *you* to find them! I should have known!"

He lunged. But not at Lucy. At Joe. With the torch held high in one hand, he brought his other fist up beneath Joe's chin. The impact jarred through Joe's skull. He staggered backwards and fell.

Pinpricks of light danced in front of his eyes. Something sharp dug into his back. He reeled with shock. The blow had come completely out of the blue. He hadn't even seen Tobias look at him! Something warm trickled out of his mouth. He put his hand to his lips. Blood.

Tobias had seized Lucy by the hair and was dragging her away. "You poisoned the household against me!" he screamed at her. "All those lies you told about me! I'll make you pay for that!"

Lucy struggled wildly, writhing and kicking out. But Tobias held her tightly at arm's length.

"We'll see if your family was lucky," he said. "If your house is still standing, you can start by showing me where you hid my papers." He gave her hair a wrench with his wrist.

Lucy cried out.

Joe scrabbled to his feet. His head was still spinning and he felt sick. But there was no hissing in his ears. He stumbled to catch Tobias up.

The older boy whirled round. "Stay back, demon!" he commanded, brandishing the flaming torch. "We all know what fire can do! Her hair would go up in seconds. In fact, shall we try it, and see?" He moved the flame towards Lucy's temple.

"No!" Joe shouted. "Don't hurt her!" He backed away, holding up both hands. There had to be a way of rescuing Lucy from Tobias. But he stood no chance of winning, unarmed, against the other boy's firebrand.

Tobias snorted, but he let the torch fall to his side. He jerked Lucy round once more and set off across the ruins, hauling her along beside him.

Joe followed, flinching when Lucy whimpered. For the first time, he wondered if it might actually be best if Lucy's house *had* burnt down. Then the plans would have gone and Tobias wouldn't be able to get them back.

But of course, that wouldn't help. If the plans had been destroyed, Tobias could deny that he'd ever plotted to kill the King. He could even do it again, if he chose. Lucy would have risked everything for nothing.

No, it would be better if the house still stood. But Lucy would have to convince Tobias that the plans had gone with the family's possessions. Could she do that? Could she keep up the lie if Tobias threatened her? Joe wasn't sure.

Nobody challenged Tobias as he forced Lucy across the wasteland towards what remained of Threadneedle Street. Not one of the people they passed even looked up. Were they blind? Or had they seen and lost so much that their senses were deadened?

Tobias and Lucy had disappeared by the time Joe reached the first of the houses. He'd watched them closely enough to know which street they had taken. But they were now nowhere to be seen. They must have gone into Lucy's house.

Panic mounted inside Joe. How could he tell which one it was?

Then he remembered following Tobias across Jorvik one snowy night. It was strange to think of it in the glowing ruins of another world. But he remembered that he and Lucy hadn't known for certain that Tobias was there until they saw his tracks in the snow. There should be tracks here too, not on the road, where the ash had been trodden down, but through the drift along the edge.

He made himself walk slowly so he could scrutinise the ground in front of each building. It was almost impossible to concentrate when every nerve and sinew in him was screeching at him to hurry, hurry, hurry!

The first building was no more than half a house. A four-poster bed teetered on the edge of what remained of the upstairs floor. Its canopy hung in charred shreds. Further along was the first whole house, followed by the second. The plaster between the beams was as black as the beams themselves, but the ash was undisturbed at the foot of both houses. Nobody had returned here yet.

But at the door to the third house, the ash had been trampled. Joe's pulse quickened. This was exactly what he'd hoped to find. Yet he was afraid, too.

For a second, he stood looking up at the front of the house. It must be Lucy's house, surely, but he couldn't see Tobias' flame through either of the downstairs windows. He prayed Tobias hadn't already dragged Lucy into the kitchen.

Just then, he saw a movement through the sitting room window. He rubbed one of the diamond panes with his cuff and peered in. The room was in deep gloom. He screwed up his eyes, trying to make out what the movement might have been. His pulse was throbbing. Perhaps he'd imagined it. There was nothing at all in the room, as far as he could see.

Then the movement came again, a shadow darting along the floor beside the wall. Joe cleaned a second pane of glass and put his face right up to it this time, shielding his eyes. In the back corner, a dark bundle was hunched on the ground.

In a flash, he knew what it was. His heartbeat

stilled for a moment and his mind ran clear. He saw, with absolute certainty, how he could use this. This could be his weapon!

Very quietly, he let himself in through the front door. The door to the dining room stood open, but he could hear Tobias in the room opposite the kitchen. Joe winced at the menace in Tobias' voice. He stepped into the sitting room, and shut the door quickly behind him.

"Solomon," he whispered. "It's me, Joe."

He crept across the room towards the dark shape. "You can come out of your corner," he murmured. "I won't hurt you."

The monkey sat motionless. Joe held his breath. If Solomon took fright or screeched, Tobias would know at once that he was in the house.

A few feet away, he stopped and stretched out his hand. "It's okay," he whispered. "The fire's gone. It's alright now."

He waited for Solomon to bare his teeth or bound away, but the monkey did neither. Joe inched closer. The animal's eyes were huge in his tiny face. He'd been so mischievous before, Joe had forgotten how sweet he could look.

He reached out further, expecting any moment to be bitten or scratched. But his fingers touched soft fur. Beneath them, he felt the flutter of a heartbeat as rapid as a bird's wing. To his astonishment, a tiny hand closed around his thumb.

Joe lifted Solomon into his arms. The monkey clung to him. As he tiptoed to the door, he mumbled soothing noises into Solomon's fur. His own heart was thudding again. He hoped the sound of it wouldn't frighten the monkey. On the other hand, it might be better if Solomon was afraid. He was so meek now, Joe feared his plan might not work.

From the hallway came thumping and scuffling noises, and then a muffled curse. Joe heard Lucy cry out again. He tensed, waiting for the door to open. But Tobias dragged Lucy into the dining room.

Joe knew he had no more than a few seconds before Tobias came across the hall. He took a deep breath. All he had on his side was the element of surprise, and the hope that the monkey would remember Tobias.

Silently, he pulled the sitting room door open.

"Ready?" he murmured to Solomon. "Right, then. This is it!"

He charged across the hall into the room opposite.

"Let her go!" he yelled.

Lucy screamed. Tobias froze. And Solomon leapt, just as Joe had hoped.

It couldn't have taken even half a second, but Joe felt as though he watched in slow motion as the monkey sailed through the air. Solomon's arms and legs were outstretched, like a skydiver in free-fall. Then he struck Tobias hard, full in the face. At once, he wrapped his limbs around Tobias' head, and began to bite him.

Tobias dropped the torch to grapple with Solomon. Lucy tore herself free and staggered to the other side of the room, where she collapsed, shaking.

Joe ran to her. "Are you alright?" He bent down to help her up. But she was waving her arms, shouting incoherently.

He looked over his shoulder. The end of the room was on fire!

Joe spun round. Tobias must have kicked the torch as he wrestled with Solomon. It had rolled into the palliasses that were still on the floor. Already, knee-high flames were crackling across the straw.

"No!" Joe cried. "The house can't burn down now! It survived the Fire!"

He struggled out of his coat and threw it over the flames. They flared out around it. He hadn't spread it wide enough! He gritted his teeth and picked it up by the edge, intending to fling it down again. But lifting it caused a draught that fanned the fire. More orange tongues sprang up, strong and hungry.

He let the coat fall. Straight away, fire began to lick at the cuffs.

He scoured the room for something else, anything! But there was nothing! In desperation, he began to stamp at the edge of the blaze. Scraps of the palliasse covers came away, turned black and died. Vivid stems of straw dulled and went out. He stamped further in. Ash crumbled beneath his foot. But the fire was still growing faster than he could stifle it!

Something snagged his shoe. He shook it. Part of the cover had got caught around the toe. A fresh thread of smoke rose into the air. The shoe was smouldering.

He shook his foot harder. He couldn't get the shoe free. In a moment, it would catch fire! He had to get it off!

Balancing on his other foot, he stooped and grasped the heel. The shoe slipped off easily, but he couldn't free it from the tangle. He would have to drop it and let it burn.

The heat of the fire beat against his face. He shied away. To his horror, he felt himself lose his balance. He tried to hop on his remaining shoe. The heel turned over. He started to fall.

There was nothing for it. He put his stockinged foot down in the burning palliasse. There was a smell of scorching hair as the stocking caught light. Then the flames were racing across his foot. For a moment, the pain was so shocking, he couldn't move.

With an immense effort, he stumbled clear of the fire and crumpled down on the floor. He clasped his foot with both hands, trying vainly to deaden the pain.

There was a sudden gust of wind. The fire roared. A figure burst into the room.

16

It was Ellen.

"Sand!" she cried. "Get the sand from the kitchen!"

She surveyed the room: Joe curled up on the floor clutching his foot, Lucy pressed back against the far wall, away from the fire and away from Tobias, who was still trying to wrest himself free from Solomon. The monkey seemed determined not to let go. He was probably enjoying himself far too much to give it up, Joe thought.

"Hurry up!" Ellen shouted.

Joe wondered if she was shouting at him or Lucy. Then he heard rumbling in the hallway, and the sound of someone straining against something heavy. The barrel rolled into the room, pushed by Lucy's brother.

"There's no time to lose!" Ellen cried. She wrenched the lid off the barrel, while it still lay on its side, and began scooping out handfuls of sand and scattering them over the fire.

But the flames had really taken hold now. The sand made no difference.

"Isn't there a shovel?" Peter dashed out of the room.

He must have opened the back door because the fire flared again. Flames licked up the wooden wall panels. They began to burn.

A few moments later, Peter ran back in. Ellen leaned to one side as he plunged the shovel into the barrel.

Joe watched him throw a huge heap of sand over the fire. A long, dark shape tumbled through the air. Joe's head was too fuzzy with pain to recognise it.

"Joe! Quick!" There was urgency in Lucy's voice.

Tobias heard it too. With one final contortion, he ripped Solomon off him and hurled him into a corner.

In the middle of the fire, poking out of the sand, was a roll of papers.

Joe sprang forward. The pain in his foot was excruciating! A wisp of smoke appeared as the papers began to burn.

From the other side of the room, Tobias also launched himself towards the fire.

Joe's fingertips brushed against the roll. It slid away from his grip. He couldn't bear to leap into the flames. He grasped again, stretching every muscle so much it hurt. The papers were dry and warm to the touch, and slightly gritty. He seized them and whipped them out.

Tobias charged at him.

Joe staggered clear of the fire. He wished he had something to hold Tobias at bay.

In the split-second before Tobias was upon him, he flung the papers towards Lucy. Tobias twisted in the air to catch them, missed, and slammed into Joe.

The back of Joe's head hit the floor. Nausea heaved in his stomach. Dizziness swirled behind his eyes. He waited for the hissing. But again, it didn't come.

With every ounce of his strength, he shoved Tobias off him and scrambled to his feet, ready to defend himself as best he could.

But Ellen stood over Tobias. There was a knife in her hand.

"What is the meaning of all this?" she exploded.

Tobias didn't answer.

"What *was* that object? What could be so important that you would kidnap my daughter and burn down my house, just to get your hands on it?"

Hatred flashed in Tobias' eyes. Joe watched his gaze flick towards Lucy, who held the papers in both hands. The room was growing more gloomy by the second, as Peter shovelled sand over the fire, putting it out. Would Tobias risk making a grab for the papers in the half-light?

But Ellen saw it too. She thrust the point of the

knife right up to Tobias' throat. "Does my blade have to touch your skin," she growled, "before you find a civil tongue and answer me?"

Joe held his breath. Lucy's mother had seemed so gentle. But there was little doubt that she was ready to use the knife if she had to.

"It was *him*!" Tobias jabbed his finger at Joe. "He might look ordinary to you, but he's a demon!"

"He's not!" cried Lucy. "He's nothing of the sort!"

"He's an evil spirit!" snarled Tobias. "I've seen him disappear into thin air!"

"So have I!" retorted Lucy. "But unlike you, he *isn't* evil. He's done nothing but good!" Her anger had given her fresh courage. She stepped forward, flushed with fury. "*He* wanted to stop the fire that's destroyed London. If I'd listened to him properly, we might have prevented it! But at least we stopped *you* from killing the King!"

"What is all this?" Ellen's face was still taut with rage, but she looked bewildered too.

"That night," Lucy said, "the night we met Joe on the way back from Foxhall, Tobias didn't drag him out of the house. What I told you wasn't quite the truth." She dropped her gaze under her mother's fierce stare. "Joe and I heard Tobias go out. We followed him together."

With her finger, she smoothed the black ribbon that was tied around the papers. "He was meeting some other apprentices in secret. We heard him talking about his plan to set fire to the Palace of Whitehall, and to Westminster and the Tower! That's what's written in these papers." She held up the roll. "Joe distracted him so that I had time to get back here and find them."

"This all happened before you woke us?" Ellen didn't look as though she quite believed her daughter.

Lucy nodded. "I couldn't think where to hide them so I buried them in the sand. Then I came to wake you so that you'd catch Tobias letting himself back in. I wanted you to know he'd been out. And I was fairly sure Joe wouldn't be with him."

"He vanished right in front of me," screeched Tobias, "just like I told you!" He had managed to edge away from Ellen's knife towards the door.

Ellen looked at Joe. "That's impossible!"

"No, it's true," Joe said.

"It is," Lucy added.

Ellen shook her head in disbelief. "What about the rest of it?" She rounded on Tobias again. He cowered away from her knife. "Did *you* start this great fire we've just suffered?" Ellen asked. "After all, you did disappear the day it broke out."

"It wasn't me!" Tobias said with venom. "But London deserved every spark that fell on her! I never knew a more godless city, every one of you heedless of the Lord's commandments, taken up with your own pleasure! I only wish this house had burned with the rest!"

Ellen gasped. Her eyes were wide with outrage. "I've half a mind to kill you here and now," she said in a low voice. Her knuckles were white around the handle of the knife. "It would be easy enough. You'd be just another casualty of the fire. No-one would even ask after you!"

The colour drained from Tobias' cheeks. "You wouldn't! You wouldn't want blood on your hands!" But he didn't sound certain.

"Why not? You'd have had the blood of royalty and government on yours, the heart's blood of the nation! We both know what the King would do with you if he heard of your intentions. Why shouldn't I do it now and save him the trouble?"

There was absolute silence.

After several long seconds, Ellen answered her own question. "Because I'm a better human being than you," she said. "That's why not. I *choose* not to do it. So go! Go, now! Get out of my house, and *never* return!"

She stepped back to let Tobias get to his feet. "Just remember, we will keep your plans amongst our most treasured possessions. If I ever see you again, or hear that you've been making mischief, then depend upon it, I will take the plans straight to the Palace."

Tobias turned in the doorway. His face was still white, but malice glittered in his eyes. "As you wish, madam," he said icily. "But I prefer to depend upon the Lord, and upon the knowledge that you will all burn in hell!" With that, he turned once more, and left.

For several long moments, everyone looked at the empty doorway.

Then Ellen put the knife down on the windowsill and went to Lucy. She took the roll of papers from her hand. "I'll look at these later," she said, "but you're alive! Oh, Lucy!" Her voice was full of warmth again. She hugged her daughter to her. "I thought I'd lost you! I'm so happy you're alright! You're not hurt?"

"No." Lucy smiled, though her eyes shone with tears. "I'm fine. But I think Joe might have burned himself. He found me in the ruins and was bringing me back here. When Tobias saw us and dragged me away, Joe came to rescue me. But the palliasses caught light. He tried to put the fire out. He was so brave! I should have thought of the sand. I knew it was here, of course I knew! That's why I turned back when we were trying to get away. To get the plans from the barrel."

"Why didn't you tell us about Tobias?" Ellen asked softly. "You seem to have managed to stop him. But that was an awful responsibility to bear alone."

"It wasn't just me," Lucy said. "I had Joe, when he was here."

Ellen turned to look at him. She raised an inquisitive eyebrow. "What is all this about you disappearing?"

Joe sighed. "I think you might see for yourself quite soon, madam," he said, wishing it were not true. "I really did vanish in front of Tobias, and in front of Lucy before that."

Ellen frowned.

"Lucy can explain to you later," Joe said. He hobbled across the room to his friend. "I haven't got long now," he said to her. "I know this from the other times. I'll be gone in a few minutes at most. Oh, Lucy!" He bit his lip.

"Is the pain very bad?" She put a hand on his arm.

Joe looked down at the floor and blinked. "It's not that," he said. His voice was thick. "When I go this time, we won't ever see each other again."

Lucy was crestfallen. "Are you sure?"

"Well, you won't see me. I'll see you, but it will be another world, and you won't remember me, so it won't be the same." He took both her hands and held them tight.

"But I didn't forget you while you were gone these last three times," she said.

"That was different," he replied. "I knew I'd be coming back. But this time, it really is goodbye." He looked into her eyes.

"Can't we do something to stop it?" she pleaded. "I thought you disappeared when you were in danger. And you *have* been in danger, from Tobias and from this fire here. But you didn't disappear. And now you're safe! Everything is going to be alright – as long as my father …" She faltered and looked at Ellen.

"Don't worry about him," Ellen said. "He's well. He's meeting us here shortly. He'd gone to make more enquiries. He was still trying to find you. But I know he'll agree that Joe is just as welcome to stay as he's always been." She smiled wryly.

"Please Joe! Won't you stay?" Lucy begged. "It's been so short. But you've done so much to help us! At least stay until my father comes!"

Joe shook his head miserably. "I can't." Already, he could hear the distant hissing in his ears. "I need you to give me my St. Christopher back," he said.

She dug her hand into her skirts and brought it out. "If I give you this, there's no way for you to get back, is there? You said this was the key."

He nodded. "But if you don't give it to me, I'll never see you again in any world!" The hissing was growing steadily louder. "Quick, Lucy! Please give it to me! Who knows? Maybe you *will* remember me next time!"

"You know, I think I will," she said earnestly. "I feel as though the fire has burned every moment of our time into my memory. I'm sure I'll never forget you!" She put the St. Christopher into his hand.

The chain trickled across Joe's palm. He looked down at the disk. It felt flat and smooth, and so familiar. He should tell Lucy that he hadn't meant what he'd just said, that he knew there was no way she'd remember him next time. He'd only said it to get her to give the St. Christopher back.

The hissing swelled, filling his ears. The room began to fade. Or perhaps it was kinder to leave it like that, to leave her with some hope. No, he thought, he couldn't finish on a lie. She should know the truth, the whole truth. "Lucy -" He hesitated. "Lucy, you do know, I …"

But she was gone. Ellen and Peter were gone, and so was the house with the heap of ash and sand on the floor, and the monkey in the corner of the room. Joe realised with a rush of guilt that he hadn't even checked whether Solomon was hurt. He had used Solomon, risked the monkey's life in order to save Lucy.

Lucy.

He gulped. He'd nearly said something he really shouldn't, the sort of thing you didn't say to a friend. He hadn't even known he was going to say it until he started to speak. It was just as well he'd faded out. Though maybe it was different if you knew you'd never see the person again.

He pulled his duvet up over his head. He felt sick and dizzy. That was why his eyes watered.

After a while, he kicked the duvet off again. It was too hot and his pillow was damp. Then he remembered about his foot. It didn't hurt. Back in Lucy's world, the pain had been acute.

He sat up and turned the light on. Across the bridge of his foot was a patch of skin that was smoother than the rest. It was a strange shape. It reminded him of the golden pheasant on Lucy's house sign.

He turned the light off and lay down again. In the darkness, he explored each of his scars with his fingertips: the tiny circle in his thigh from the point of the sharpened stylus, the tear in his side from the narwhal horn, the triangular scar where the arrow tip had entered his shoulder. And now the bird-like shape of the burn on his foot.

He wasn't ready yet to think about the next time. There would be a next time, he presumed. He didn't know what he would do if one day, there wasn't. But in any case, this world was still too fresh to think about it at the moment.

How extraordinary, he thought, that he'd actually seen the Great Fire of London! It had been more horrifying than he could ever have imagined. But now that he knew Lucy was safe, he no longer felt sick at the thought of it.

Of course, although she had survived, and her family and home had survived too, life wasn't going to go back to normal for her for a long time, if ever. The winter rains would fall on the embers, and she would be living for months at least, perhaps years, on the edge of blackened ruins. But eventually, the city would rise again. This wouldn't be the first time it had to be reborn. Nor would it be the last.

He still felt a nagging sense of disappointment that he and Lucy hadn't managed to stop the fire. He'd known all along that it would be impossible. But he couldn't help wondering if it would have been different if he'd been there on the night it broke out.

On the other hand, he consoled himself, they had stopped Tobias doing something far, far worse. London might be nothing more than a forest of chimney stacks in a sea of ash. But England still had a king and a government. If Tobias' plot had worked, none of that would have survived.

Sleep started to creep up on Joe. There was so much still to think about. He fought to stay awake. But his eyelids were heavy. He turned over in bed and drew his knees up to his chest so that he could reach the smooth patch on his foot.

"Goodnight, Lucy," he murmured. "And Lucy, you know, I -" But even though he was alone, he couldn't bring himself to say out loud the words he'd nearly said to her. So he thought them instead.

And maybe, he thought, *just maybe, you might remember me when we meet again*. He didn't believe it, but it comforted him. It was something to hold on to for now.

Until the next time.

THE END